Something abo
Julie to draw closer, to know him
better.

That was something she couldn't afford. Especially after learning his wife had lied to him.

"It's late. I need to go," she told him.

He followed her to the door. She looked up at him, resisting the impulse to reach up and touch his cheek to ease his worry. "Go up and say good-night to your daughter, Gil. And relax. All you need to do is show Abby you love her," she advised.

Julie fought tears all the way home. She cried for Gil, who was longing for his child's love, and for herself, for bringing another lie into the Montgomerys' life. What a mess this was.

Thankfully, tomorrow was her last day. She'd have to pray that Gil's mother could guide the pair to a new relationship. But in her heart she knew she was the only one who could do that. She had a bond with Abby neither of them had.

Biology. Blood *was* thicker than water.

Lorraine Beatty was raised in Columbus, Ohio, but now calls Mississippi home. She and her husband, Joe, have two sons and five grandchildren. Lorraine started writing in junior high and is a member of RWA and ACFW, and is a charter member and past president of Magnolia State Romance Writers. In her spare time she likes to work in her garden, travel and spend time with her family.

Books by Lorraine Beatty

Love Inspired

Home to Dover

Protecting the Widow's Heart
His Small-Town Family
Bachelor to the Rescue
Her Christmas Hero
The Nanny's Secret Child

Rekindled Romance
Restoring His Heart

The Nanny's Secret Child

Lorraine Beatty

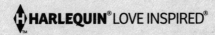

Recycling programs for this product may not exist in your area.

™ LOVE INSPIRED BOOKS

ISBN-13: 978-0-373-71950-1

The Nanny's Secret Child

www.Harlequin.com

Printed in U.S.A.

Therefore each of you must put off falsehood
and speak truthfully to your neighbor,
for we are all members of one body.
—*Ephesians* 4:25

To my mother-in-law, Mary.
My biggest fan and my dearest friend.
What a blessing you are to us.

Chapter One

"Turn right onto Sycamore Avenue. Your destination is on the right."

Julianna Bishop followed the directions on her GPS and made the turn, searching the house numbers for 122. The old, established neighborhood in Dover, Mississippi, could have been lifted from a fifties television sitcom. Each home oozed charm, their appealing facades nestled on neatly landscaped yards that even the gray drab of January couldn't dim. Full-grown trees stripped of their leaves arched overhead, filtering the bright sunlight streaming down from a clear blue sky. Evergreen live oaks and giant magnolia trees added a splash of green to the winter landscapes.

The peaceful and picturesque surroundings were at odds with the violent storm raging inside her. She swallowed hard against the tightness in her throat and searched the house numbers again. Heart pounding against her rib cage, Julie pressed down on the brakes, bringing the car to a full stop. She had arrived. One-twenty-two Sycamore Avenue was a two-story white colonial with black shutters, a red front door and a lamppost at the edge of the sidewalk. Her hands gripped the steering wheel, turning her knuckles white. She was doing the right thing. Her prayers had been answered.

Her gaze surveyed the white house more closely. It was exactly as she'd expected. It was a beautiful home, the kind of place where families laughed and loved and enjoyed each other. All that was missing was the white picket fence.

Closing her eyes, Julie inhaled slowly, hoping to settle her jittery nerves. The house and the neighborhood were reassuring. Everything would be fine.

Sliding the gear shift into Park, she inhaled a couple of slow breaths, hoping to calm her churning stomach and take a moment to plan her introduction. The opening strains of "Mighty God" sounded from the depths of her oversize purse. She rummaged around, found the small phone and glanced at the display. DiDi. Her moral support. And oh, how she needed her longtime best friend at this moment. "Hey."

"Are you there yet?"

DiDi's anxious tone mirrored her own. "Yes." Julie rested her head against the back of the seat, mentally scolding herself for being such a coward. "I just pulled up out front."

"I'm praying for you."

"I'm praying for me, too."

"Have you figured out what you're going to say to him?"

"Uh, I was thinking of, 'Hello. I'm the nanny.'"

"You know what I mean. What if he suspects?"

"Di, you're not helping." Julie pressed her hand against her stomach, trying to quell the nausea.

"Sorry. I know you have to do this. I just hope you find the peace you're looking for when this is over."

Her friend's loving concern and understanding did more to ease Julie's anxiety than all her prayers. She thanked the Lord every day for sending Deirdre Simmons into her life. "I know it will. The Lord's given me this chance, and I can't pass it up."

"Be careful. Watch your emotions, girlfriend. You deserve to be happy, and I hope after this you will be."

Julie ended the call, then peered out at the house again. *Lord, this is a blessing from You, isn't it? The answer to my prayers?* There was no other explanation. Why else would Gil Montgomery's name turn up at the Nanny Connection Agency, and why else would she be available to step in to fill the assignment?

The timing was too perfect to be anything other than a gift from God. She'd ended her job as a secondgrade teacher at Christmas. In three months she'd be boarding a plane for Paris and a new life as a teacher at the International School. The five-year assignment she'd dreamed about and worked toward for years. In the meantime, she continued to work as a nanny, a second job she'd held in the summers and on school holidays. The butterflies were still battling in her stomach, but she'd regained her confidence. It might be nerveracking at first, but when all was said and done, she'd have peace and she could step into her future finally free of the gnawing questions. Anticipation coursed through her like carbonated water, making her all bubbly with excitement.

Climbing out of the car, Julie tugged her sweater down, adjusted her scarf and slung her large purse over her shoulder. The walkway to the front door was long and winding, giving her the time she needed to disengage her emotions and find her professional nanny zone. This afternoon's meeting with the family was a mere formality. She'd been through it dozens of times. It was a chance for everyone involved to get a feel for one another and gauge their compatibility. It was unusual to meet on a Sunday, but given the urgency of the client's request, it was understandable.

Fingers trembling, she rang the doorbell, lifting up one more prayer. The only way this would work was to keep her heart locked away and her emotions shut down. She'd assimilate everything later when she got home. She swallowed the knot in her throat and tried to ignore the fierce pounding of her heart.

Movement from the other side of the small panes in the front door froze her breath in her lungs. This was a happy assignment. Joyous, even. She would concentrate on that. She pasted a smile on her face as the door clicked open. The man in the doorway stared back at her, looking puzzled and confused. But he wasn't the middle-aged, slightly paunchy man she'd expected. This guy was early thirties, tops. Tall, well built and with sculpted features that were drawn downward in a fierce scowl. Did she have the right house? The numbers beside the door confirmed her location.

"Yes?"

She cleared her throat. "I'm from the Nanny Connection Agency. You requested a nanny?" His frown deepened, and he scanned her quickly with intense cobalt blue eyes. A gust of wind blew hair across her face, and she raked it way with her fingertips and widened her smile.

"Right." The man touched his forehead and nod-

ded, motioning her inside. "Forgive me. I didn't realize what time it was."

Julie stepped into the foyer, her gaze quickly scanning the small entry. Outdated wallpaper covered the
walls, and a shiny brass chandelier hung from the ceil-
ing. The stairs were covered with worn carpet and the
parquet floors had seen better days.

"Thanks for coming. I'm Gil Montgomery." He extended his hand.

She grasped it, her fingers enveloped in a strong,
warm grip, along with a snap of static electricity as if
she'd rubbed her feet across new carpet before touch-
ing him. Or had she imagined it? It was winter after
all, and the air was dry. She looked up into his eyes and
found it hard to look away. She saw intelligence and
probing, and a swell of appreciation rolled along her
nerves. He was a very attractive man. She blinked and
smiled. "Julie Bishop." He motioned her to follow him.

Glimpses of the other rooms as she passed by left
her puzzled. The interior of the home didn't match
the picture-perfect exterior. The layout was small and
cramped, and the scale of the furniture was all wrong.
Oversize and ornate, it was better suited for a much
larger and more modern home. The rooms were relics
from the eighties. The disjointed feel about the house
added another flip to her churning stomach. She'd envisioned the inside of the home as warm and welcoming, filled with antiques and lovingly worn furniture.
Not these conflicted styles. What did that say about
the people who lived here?

Like Gil Montgomery.

Her gaze landed on the broad back of the man. He
wasn't supposed to be this elegantly handsome man

who moved with athletic grace and control. He was a head taller than her, which placed him a little over six feet in height. The dark blue knit shirt tucked in neatly at the narrow waist hung nicely over his broad shoulders. She continued her inventory as she followed behind him. A head of wavy, coffee-brown hair curled slightly over his ears and along the nape of his neck, suggesting he was in need of a trim. But it was the eyes that had grabbed her full attention. They were a rich cobalt blue, with long dark lashes and tiny crinkles at the corners. Julie dismissed the idle thoughts. What the man looked like was neither here nor there. She closed her eyes and offered up one more prayer.

"Oomph."

Her face bumped into a wall of muscle when Mr. Montgomery stopped in the kitchen. Her hands rested against a solid back. Warmth from beneath his shirt transferred to her palms, sending a funny squiggle into her stomach. She dropped her hand and stepped back. His dark blue eyes held concern.

"Sorry. Are you all right? I didn't realize you were so close behind me."

She nodded and stepped back quickly, uncomfortable with the sensations coursing through her at his nearness. "My fault. I was distracted by…" *you.* "Your home, it's charming."

He raised an eyebrow. "It's a chopped-up mess."

He'd stopped in a large and sunny breakfast nook. This part of the house had a warmer and friendlier feel, though the furniture was still all wrong. The glass-topped table didn't fit with the country kitchen, which though charming, was a couple of decades out of date with the light oak cabinets, laminate countertops and almond appliances. Placing her purse on the table, she glanced over her shoulder to find her new employer staring at her. His dark blue eyes narrowed and a deep frown creased his high forehead. Her pulse jumped. What did he see? She forced a smile, her hand went to her throat, her fingers wrapping around the small heart necklace she always wore, trying to calm the sense of being exposed.

"You're younger than I expected."

Julie expelled a soft breath. She'd heard this before. "Is that a problem?"

He rubbed his temple with two fingers. "I've never hired a nanny before. I was expecting someone more mature. How long have you been doing this? Being a nanny, I mean?"

Typical questions. She was used to them. She smiled reassuringly, trying to ignore the anticipation that was swirling in her stomach now that she was actually here. She only hoped he wouldn't send her away. "I'm a teacher by profession. Second grade. But I've worked as a nanny during summers and holidays for the last six years."

Mr. Montgomery nodded, the worry lines in his forehead deepening. Had she come here only to be dismissed because she wasn't gray-haired and over fifty?

"I'm sure you're qualified, or you wouldn't be working for the agency." He gestured for her to be seated at the table, then joined her, clasping his hands on the top. "I wanted to take a minute to talk about my daughter before I introduce you."

"I'm looking forward to meeting her." She was surprised she could even speak around the tightness in her throat. He held her gaze, sending her heart pounding again. Could he sense her turmoil? Was the truth written in her eyes? Her false smile? Or was she being paranoid?

"Abby has been through a lot these last six months. Her mother's illness and death were hard on her. I brought her back here to be close to my family. My mother has been taking care of her since Christmas, but she had to leave the country suddenly."

Julie tamped down the pain in her heart and schooled her features. This wasn't going the way she'd expected. What did he mean "brought her back"? "Abby wasn't with you?"

Montgomery set his jaw a moment before continuing. "She went to live with her mother in Mobile after the divorce. But she's with me now and that's all that matters."

She nodded, unable to speak. Everything was all wrong. She wished she'd read his application more closely. She'd seen where he'd recently lost his wife, but not that he was divorced. She fought to remain composed. "It's hard for a child to lose a parent, especially at a young age. I imagine she's having trouble adjusting to the change?"

Montgomery glanced away briefly before meeting her gaze. "Yes. She was just getting comfortable here with my mom and now another change." He rubbed his temple. "I don't want her to be any more upset."

"When will your mother be home again?"

"She's supposed to return next week. My sister is a dancer. She was performing in London and had an accident. Mom flew over to be with her until she can travel." He pushed away from the table and stood. "I wanted you to know what to expect. I'm not sure how she'll react to this new development."

"I understand. As a teacher I've dealt with all types of children and their challenges. I'm sure it'll be fine, but I appreciate you telling me." She could see Mr. Montgomery relax slightly, as if a burden was lifted from his shoulders. Unfortunately it had shifted onto hers. Had the mother's death been so traumatic? Was her father providing the love and support his child needed? She forced her thoughts off that track. One step at a time. One minute at a time.

Montgomery met her gaze. "She means everything to me. I want only the best for her. I'm sure you understand."

The sincerity and concern in his tone eased much of her worry. It was clear that he loved his daughter. Montgomery's cell buzzed. He slipped it from his pocket, excused himself, moving to the other end of the kitchen. She heard him say something about breaker boxes before ending the call.

"Other than giving your full attention to Abby, you won't have any other duties. The housekeeper, Mrs. Fontenot, comes on Friday. I'd like you to be here early enough to fix breakfast and take Abby to school in the morning and pick her up each day. I'll be home in time to handle supper, but I'd like you to be available at all times while she's at school just in case."

"That's fine. I have plenty to keep me occupied. I tutor older students online, and I'm moving to Paris in a few months so there's lots of paperwork involved."

"France. Sounds interesting. I meant to ask where you live. Is it a long commute to Dover?"

"Not too bad. I live in Brandon, east of Jackson. It takes about forty-five minutes."

He nodded. "I'd prefer you were closer. But if for some reason you need to stay late or be here early, there's a mother-in-law suite down the hall from Abby's room. There's also a small furnished apartment above the garage you can use."

"I'll remember that. But I'm an early riser, so the commute isn't a problem."

Montgomery rubbed his jaw, then rested his hands on his hips. "I think that covers everything. I'll get Abby, and you two can get acquainted."

Julie kept the smile on her face until Montgomery disappeared into the hallway, then lowered her head into her hands. What had she gotten into? Her fight-or-flight instinct was raging. Heart pounding. Veins burning. Stomach in knots. Her common sense screamed run! But her heart ached to stay and face her fear once and for all. She had to know. Once she had that reassurance to hold on to, she could face the future.

Gil Montgomery strode down the hallway, puzzling over the new nanny. She was not what he'd expected. At first glance he'd thought she was a teenager in her jeans, loose sweater and big scarf. All that had been missing was a cell phone clutched in her hand. But a closer look revealed a woman near his age, with a rosy complexion and a smile bright enough to light up a room, though he'd seen a hint of anxiety in her big brown eyes. The wind had lifted her hair, sending wavy strands across her cheek, and wrapped him in a faint scent of spring.

Spring was a long way off. Glancing down at his

hand, he lightly rubbed his thumb over his palm. Had he imagined that jolt to his system when he'd taken her hand? Judging from her expression, he suspected she'd felt it, too. Odd. It had sparked like static, the way it had when he and his brother used to slide their feet across the carpet then zap each other. Except that they hadn't crossed any carpet.

Of course, her looks were immaterial. Her credentials were what mattered, and they looked exemplary. He was being overprotective. Hiring a nanny had him on edge. He wasn't sure he liked the idea of a younger and very attractive nanny for Abby. He'd feel better with a more matronly woman, someone who could devote all her attention to his daughter. Unfortunately he didn't have a choice. Until his mother returned, he'd have to rely on this woman to care for his only child.

At the top of the stairs he stopped at Abby's door. He wanted to pray, to ask the Lord to help his little girl, but he'd prayed for three years and nothing had changed. That wasn't God's fault. That was all on him.

He tapped lightly on the door, then peeked in. Abby was curled up on her bed looking at a book, her ever-present gray-and-pink polka-dot backpack at her side. His heart swelled, pressing against his rib cage. Every part of her was perfect, from her sweet little face with her big brown eyes to the sprinkle of freckles across her button nose.

He finally had her back, and from now on he'd be part of her life. A knot formed in the center of his chest. He'd missed so many of her milestones. It had cost him nearly every penny he possessed to gain custody of her and bring her back home to Dover. He would have spent twice that to have her with him again.

But to Abby, he was a stranger. He was the father who never came to visit, who never called or sent gifts. He had, of course, but interference from his ex-wife and her meddling sister had driven a wedge between him and his daughter. Now she was home, but she was withdrawn and sad and he had no idea how to help her.

He approached the bed, putting a big smile on his face. "Hey, pumpkin."

She looked over at him, her expression devoid of any emotion. "I'm not a pumpkin."

She'd started to smile under his mother's care, but now she'd have to adjust to the nanny. So much change so quickly. "I know you're not. Your grandpa used to call my sisters pumpkin. It was his special name for his little girls. I want to have a special name for you. Like ladybug or cricket."

Abby closed her book. "I'm not a bug either."

The words were spoken with little feeling, sending a shard of pain through his heart. He wanted to fill the void left by her mother's death, but he had no idea how to do that. He came from a large family, two brothers and two sisters, so he should know what to do, but he'd missed too much of his daughter's life. She wasn't a baby now. She was a young girl, almost nine, with a mind of her own, and she wasn't happy to be here with him.

Discouraged, Gil nodded. "Right, well, the nanny is here. You ready to meet her?"

Abby shrugged and got to her feet, picking up her backpack. When she drew near, he reached out and touched the top of her head, stroking the soft brown hair. She stepped out of his reach, rebuffing his touch and plunging a hot blade into his heart.

Closing his eyes, he offered up a quick prayer. Maybe this time the Lord would hear and take action because he was out of options. *Please, Lord, help my little girl find joy again. I don't know what to do for her.*

His thoughts circled back to the new nanny as he followed his daughter downstairs. She was young, pretty and capable. He'd seen a spark in her eyes that intrigued him. Anticipation? As a teacher and a nanny, she obviously liked kids. Maybe having a younger woman in her life would be a good thing for Abby. He wasn't so sure having her in his home would be good for him. He didn't like the way he was drawn to her bright smile and sparkling eyes. Or the inappropriate questions that burst into his mind. Like was she involved with anyone?

At the bottom of the stairs he stopped and touched Abby's shoulder. "Remember. Be polite." She glared up at him, screwed up her mouth and walked on.

Maybe the nanny could do what he couldn't—make Abby happy again.

Julie paced the kitchen, waiting for father and child to return, struggling to keep her professional mask in place against the questions and doubts. Her gaze drifted to the bay window in the breakfast room and the wooden deck overlooking the large backyard, where a swing hung from a branch of an old tree. She bit her bottom lip in delight. She could imagine her little charge swinging once the weather broke. But she wouldn't be here to see that. Her assignment was only for a week. Five days in which to learn the answers to her questions.

Mr. Montgomery's deep voice sounded from the

hall. Julie braced, her entire body vibrating. Would he see? Would he know? No time for further speculation. They were here. She smiled, her heart in her throat. The moment had arrived, and she had no idea what to expect.

Montgomery rested one hand on his daughter's shoulder as he stood behind her. "Miss Bishop, this is my daughter, Abby."

She barely heard him. Her eyes were on her new charge. She was a beautiful child. Long dark brown hair fell below her shoulders, held back with clips on each side, revealing little pink ears and soft rosy cheeks. Big brown eyes stared back at her. "Hello, Abby."

"Hello."

The reply was uttered with little enthusiasm. Not surprising. Accepting a new caregiver took a period of adjustment. Unfortunately, there wouldn't be much time for that. For the next few days she'd merely be a highly paid babysitter. But it would be worth it.

Julie moved forward and extended her hand. "I'm…" She cleared her throat. "I'm happy to meet you." The little girl clutched the faded backpack, staring up at her with a dull gaze. Julie glanced at the father. He looked worried and a bit sad. She remembered what he'd said about the recent upheavals in her life. "Why don't you sit down and we'll talk a moment."

Once they were settled, Julie rested her elbows on the table and peered over at Abby, examining each inch of her. From her heart-shaped face to the sprinkle of freckles across her upturned nose, she was an adorable little girl. Her pretty brown eyes were framed with long thick lashes, but as lovely as her eyes were, they lacked the spark of excitement and curiosity Julie liked to see in a child her age. Abby's demeanor read sad and uninvolved. Julie's heart lurched, forcing her to corral her emotions and focus on her assignment. "I'm looking forward to spending time together. Is there something special you like to do?"

Abby shrugged, fingering her backpack.

Julie glanced at the father. Pain and confusion drew his brows downward and caused a muscle to flex at the corner of his mouth. He had the look of a parent who had no idea how to help the child he loved. Something inside Julie softened. She directed her attention to Abby again. "I have some things I like to do with my students, so we'll try them out and see which ones you like, all right?"

"I'm not a student."

"That's true. But I'm a teacher most of the time, so I think of all my children that way."

She frowned. "You don't look like a nanny."

"Abby." Montgomery gently reprimanded his daughter.

She focused her attention on Abby. "Nannies come in all shapes and sizes. Just like children do. And you look like a very nice young lady." Julie had been angling for a smile, but all she received was a blink. But in that moment Julie saw emotions she recognized and understood. Abby was feeling disconnected and confused. "Abby is usually short for Abigail. Is that your real name?" The child shrugged again. "My name is Julianna Bishop, but everyone calls me Julie."

Abby stared back at her, little mouth pressed into a frown. "Mine is Abigail Sarah Montgomery. My mommy said Sarah means 'princess.'"

Encouraged, Julie continued. "Little girls are always princesses to their mommies…and daddies." An unexpected stab of pain penetrated her barriers. Like sand washing away with a wave, her foundation began to erode. Blood drained from her face. A surge of lightheadedness blurred her vision. She rubbed her forehead, willing herself to calm down. She glanced across the table at the little girl and felt her stomach heave.

Mr. Montgomery's cell rang again, and she grabbed the opportunity to excuse herself. "Abby, could you point me to the bathroom?"

The child gestured to the hall and Julie tried to walk, not run, from the room. Her fiercely pounding heart sent her blood roaring in her ears. She stepped into the small guest bath, shut the door and leaned against it.

She couldn't cry. Not now. She wouldn't be able to explain it. Mr. Montgomery might change his mind and ask her to leave. Or worse, he'd demand an explanation. He'd think she was unfit to care for his daughter.

Trapped in a whirlwind of colliding emotions, she fought to find her footing. Fear. Excitement. Joy. Anger. A million reactions she hadn't anticipated.

Please, please, Lord, help me. Moving to the sink, she ran cold water over her hands and pressed them to her cheeks to ease the scalding heat. Inhaling a few deep breaths, she forced herself to calm down. Slowly her stomach settled. She stared at her reflection in the mirror and saw a woman facing her worst nightmare. Not the image she wanted to project. She wanted to appear friendly and nurturing. Capable and caring. The way she seemed at school or when working as a nanny. Except this wasn't a normal assignment. Not by a long shot.

Inhaling one last calming breath, Julie straightened and turned to go. As she grasped the doorknob, the anxiety churned up again, buckling her knees. What would Gil Montgomery say if she told him the truth? That the child he called Abby was the baby girl she gave up for adoption eight years ago?

Chapter Two

With great effort, Julie managed to regain control and return to the kitchen. Mr. Montgomery looked up as she entered.

"Miss Bishop, I know you weren't supposed to start work until tomorrow, but I need to run to the office. It's only a few miles away. I was wondering if you could stay with Abby for a half hour or so. You could get better acquainted while I'm gone. Of course, I'll understand if you can't."

A million possibilities raced through her mind. What she wanted to do was run home, bury herself in bed and sort out all the emotions surging through her heart before she exploded. Yet having the chance to remain here and spend extra time with her child was a blessing she couldn't pass up, even though the danger and the potential emotional stress would be difficult.

"I'd be happy to stay. Abby can show me around, help me find things I might need."

Montgomery looked a bit leery, but nodded. "Good. Thank you." He stooped down beside Abby. "Will you be okay here with the new nanny? I won't be long."

Abby shrugged, clutching her backpack a bit closer. Montgomery raised a hand as if to stroke her hair, then let it fall, getting to his feet. The gesture caused a twinge in Julie's heart and raised a number of questions. Why was Abby so indifferent toward her father and why was he so reluctant to show his affection? Clearly there was a barrier between them. She smiled to cover her concern.

"All right, then. I shouldn't be long." He handed Julie a business card with all his numbers. "Don't hesitate to call me for anything."

"Don't worry. We'll be fine." She gave him her most reassuring smile, but the moment the door closed behind Gil Montgomery, Julie began to question her decision. Her only hope to keep from sinking into a pit of emotional quicksand was to don her professional facade, lock it down tightly and move forward. She faced Abby with her most engaging smile. "I'm feeling like a snack, how about you?"

With some assistance from Abby, Julie found plates, glasses and a tin of oatmeal cookies. After pouring two glasses of milk, she settled at the table, watching the little girl eat a cookie and take a sip of her milk. Julie took a bite of her cookie, but it turned to sawdust in her mouth. "These are really good cookies. Did you make them?" The question drew a puzzled frown from the little girl.

"My grandma made them."

"I don't think I've ever had a better one." Even though she couldn't choke one down, she had to admit they were soft, chewy and very tasty. "She must be a very good cook."

Abby shrugged again. "She had to go away."

Hope blossomed in Julie's heart. At least they were conversing now. For a while she'd feared the only source of communication would be shrugs and nods. But the resigned tone in Abby's voice bothered her. "I know. You must miss her."

One corner of the little mouth twitched upward. "Everybody goes away."

A sharp barb pricked her nerves. "But they come back. Your dad said that as soon as his sister is well, she and your grandma will come home."

"Mommy won't come home."

Julie's insides twisted at the sadness in the child's voice. She resisted the urge to scoop her up into a hug. "I'm so sorry about your mom. You must miss her very much. But you're here with your daddy now, so everything will be fine. You'll see."

Abby shoved her plate back and glared. "He doesn't want me here."

Julie stared at the little girl a moment, replaying everything she'd seen and heard since arriving at the house. If first impressions counted for anything, then Mr. Montgomery was a devoted father. The relationship between him and his daughter was strained, but she'd seen no indication that he resented his child being here. "Oh, Abby, I don't think that's true. I'm sure he loves you very much and he's happy to have you here with him."

Abby clammed up. She stared down, backpack clutched tight. Conversation over. Time to change directions. "Well, let me clean up, and then you can show me around so I won't get lost tomorrow when I come to stay with you."

"I don't need a nanny. That's for babies."

"Not always. In some countries nannies take care of children until they're all grown up."

"That's silly."

"I think you might be right. Well, why don't you think of me as a friend who will watch out for you while your daddy is at work and until your grandma comes home?"

Abby mulled that over, a frown folding her little forehead. "What do I call you?"

"How about Miss Julie? That way it'll sound more like we're friends."

"Okay."

"Good, because I want us to become friends." Was that possible? Could she have a relationship with her child beyond that of fill-in nanny? The truth shouted inside her head, burning through her heart. *Impossible.* She wasn't even supposed to know who Abby was, let alone be here taking care of her. The truth could never come out. It would be disastrous for everyone involved. The father would be furious. He might bring charges against her or the agency. Agatha Montrose, the owner of the Nanny Connection Agency, was her friend and mentor. She'd never considered what would happen to her, not to mention Julie's own reputation, should the truth come out. But most important of all, what emotional damage would it do to Abby? A swell of anxiety crashed over her senses. She stood, struggling to hold herself together. She had to calm down. No one knew about Abby except DiDi. Julie's own parents didn't know. She'd never told them she was pregnant. Not that it would have mattered one way or the other to them.

Julie gathered up the plates and glasses, taking her time at the sink, rinsing and stacking them on the counter. Doubts about this decision bombarded her from every direction. This had seemed like a gift from God at first. She'd been convinced it was the answer to her long-uplifted prayers. But now... Slowly she wiped her hands on a towel, giving herself time to regroup.

Since the day her baby was born, she'd been plagued with one question. Not, had she done the right thing in giving her up—she'd had no choice in that regard. Alone, penniless with no one to turn to, she'd known the only future she could offer her baby girl was to give her to a couple who could provide a home, brothers and sisters, love and security.

The question that had haunted her all these years was whether or not her child was happy and well cared for. Did her adopted parents love her as much as her birth mother did? That love had been the only way she'd been able to let her go. Julie fingered the small silver heart with the birthstone in the center. The only reminder of the little girl she had given up.

DiDi had somehow managed to get the name of the adoptive parents and given it to her. She'd always known the Montgomerys had taken her child, and that they lived in Mississippi, but she'd never acted upon the knowledge. She'd never looked them up, never tried to find where they lived, believing in her heart that it was best for her baby.

Until the day Gil Montgomery's name had appeared at the agency, requesting a short-term nanny. The application stated he'd lost his wife a few months ago and he needed a temporary caregiver for his daughter. Julie carefully folded the towel, glancing over at Abby, still sitting quietly at the table. She might have resisted the need to assure herself of her child's well-being if it hadn't been for her move to Paris.

The only obstacle to her dream move was her gnawing fear. Stories about adopted children who'd been mistreated, neglected or even given up again never failed to fuel a torrent of doubt and fear in her heart. What if her baby was with a family that didn't truly love her? If Julie knew her baby was happy, in a loving environment, then she could leave the country secure in the knowledge that it had all been worth it.

Julie closed her eyes, thanking the Lord for allowing her this chance. Five days. Enough time to allay her fears, to get to know her child, to gain peace and perspective before closing the door on this part of her life forever. And this *was* a blessing from God. It had to be.

She smiled at the little girl. "Okay, I'm ready to see your house. Where do you want to start?"

Begrudgingly, Abby scooted out of her chair, nodding toward the counter. "This is the kitchen."

She chuckled. "Really?" Abby didn't laugh with her, but she did move her mouth to one side. Julie followed the little girl through the downstairs rooms, pointing out each area with little fanfare. She noticed the whole house was in need of love and attention. She had a feeling the people who lived here might have that same need. She shook off the worrisome thought. She needed to think with her head, not her heart. Abby had been in Dover only a short while, and her long-term well-being wasn't her concern. Only her day-to-day care.

Back inside, she followed Abby upstairs.

"This is my room."

Julie took a quick survey of the large space. There was something odd about the decor. The pink paint was an unusual shade, the bedspread clashed with the pillows, and the curtains were more suited for a nursery. Then it hit her. This room was decorated by a man who had no idea what a little girl's room should look like. It was not the room an eight-year-old girl would dream about. Julie looked for something positive to say. "This is a really nice room. Look at all the sunlight you get."

"It's pink. I hate pink. I like purple. My other room was purple."

"It's not hard to paint walls. I'll bet if you told your daddy that you'd rather have a purple room, he'd change it for you."

Abby tossed her backpack onto the bed, then climbed up beside it, arms crossed over her little chest. "No, he wouldn't."

She sat beside her. "What makes you say that?"

"He doesn't want to be my daddy. Aunt Pam said so."

Julie's concern rose. Was this chip on her shoulder a result of grief and being taken from her home, or was there something more behind her attitude? If this were any other assignment, Julie would just go on about her job. But this wasn't a normal situation.

"I'm sure your Aunt Pam didn't mean that. Sometimes when grown-ups are angry at each other, they say things they don't mean. Your daddy brought you to this nice house and this town so you could be close to your family. Like your grandmother. You like her, don't you?"

Abby nodded, eyes glistening.

"She'll be back very soon. In the meantime, your daddy has asked me to take very good care of you and play with you and…" *to love you*. "And I'm a professional at that kind of thing."

"What's that mean?"

"That means I'm very good at taking care of children. I have lots of things we can do that are fun. Like drawing." Maybe she could get Abby to express her feelings through pictures, a technique that had worked well for Julie in the past. "Let's go back downstairs and draw until your dad gets back." Reluctantly, the little girl followed.

Julie clutched the stair railing as she descended the steps. She and Mr. Montgomery needed to have a talk. She wanted to know what Abby had been through. If she was going to help her child, she needed to know about her past. She needed to know what… She stopped at the bottom, releasing a heavy sigh. What was she doing? She wasn't here to help Abby. She wasn't her mother, not really. She was the caregiver for a few days. Nothing more.

Blood surged in her ears like waves. But how could she ignore that Abby was an unhappy little girl? She was sad and confused and clung to her backpack like a lifeline, which showed the depth of her insecurity. And she was helpless to do anything about it. Abby needed her help. She needed love and attention, and who better to provide that than her mother?

Gil pulled into his designated parking spot and shut off the engine, swallowing around the worry clogging his throat. He'd nearly turned around three times to go back and stay with Abby. He'd been adjusting to the idea of a young attractive nanny until she'd returned to the kitchen looking pale and shaky. She'd regained her equilibrium quickly, but it left him wondering if she was sick, and questioning his decision to leave his child with a stranger.

What had surprised him was the surge of protectiveness toward the woman that had overtaken him. He'd wanted to pull her close and comfort her. He'd never felt that way before. He was obviously more stressed over this situation than he'd thought. Julie Bishop was a professional caregiver. And it was only for an hour. He couldn't be with Abby every second. His mom had warned him about being overprotective. Maybe he was, but he had a lot to make up for. Because of his ignorance, he'd sent his child to live in a world of chaos. He had to undo the damage somehow. He just didn't know how.

Inside the large building that housed Montgomery Electrical Contractors, the business his family owned, he headed for the office on the second floor. His older brother Linc was behind the desk, and the sight unleashed a wave of grief that stopped him in his tracks. Their father should be running the company, but he died suddenly last fall, leaving the family reeling. Gil had barely begun to process the loss when his ex-wife had died, and he'd been caught up in a custody tornado that hadn't ended until Christmas.

Linc looked up from the desk, a smile on his face. "I take it the new nanny worked out or you wouldn't have left Abby with her."

"She wasn't what I was expecting." Gil glanced down at his hand, unable to shake the memory of holding hers. Soft, warm and strong. He'd sensed a tension about her, but he'd also been aware of her energy. There was something stable and trustworthy about

Miss Bishop. And at the same time she was fresh and appealing. "She's young." He wasn't sure why that bothered him so much.

"How young?"

"Few years younger than me, I guess."

Linc chuckled. "Hate to tell you, bro, but that isn't so young. I'm marrying a woman about that age."

Gil managed a smile. Linc had met a wonderful woman with a young son and they were planning their wedding. "I thought she'd be more grandmotherly. But she's pretty and warm and friendly." And she had beautiful dark hair that floated around her face in soft waves, brown eyes that held a sparkle and skin that glowed.

"How pretty?"

Too late he realized his mistake. Ever since Linc had fallen in love, he was eager to have others join the party. "She's qualified. That's all that matters. I only hope she and Abby can get along until Mom gets back. This is another big change in Abby's life." He started to tell his brother about other concerns but decided against it. Linc had enough on his mind between running Montgomery Electrical and planning his future. He didn't need to shoulder Gil's problems, too. They were both treading water, trying to adjust to the loss of their father and keep the family business afloat after narrowly avoiding bankruptcy last month.

"So did you like the woman? More important, did Abby like her?"

Gil rubbed his forehead. "Yeah, I did. I have no clue what Abby thought. She won't talk to me. I think I might call the agency and have them send someone older, more like Mom."

Linc nodded. "Or you can wait and see how things go. Maybe Abby needs someone younger, more flexible."

"Maybe. I just want her happy again."

"We all do. We want you to be happy again, too, bro."

He shook his head and sat. He could never be happy until Abby was. "I'm not sure that's possible. So what is it I need to sign that couldn't wait until tomorrow? It's Sunday afternoon. You should be home watching the play-offs."

Linc shoved a folder of papers toward him. "I'd rather be, but the bids on the Westfal project are due tomorrow morning and I'm hand delivering the bid to the contractor as soon as they're signed. We can't afford to miss any opportunities if we're going to stay afloat. Oh, and I saw a couple upcoming jobs on the Dodge Reports you might want to look into."

Gil scribbled his name on the documents, then tossed the pen onto the desk. "Is that all? I need to get back to Abby."

Linc glanced at the signature, then closed the folder. "Yeah. I know I shouldn't, but I'm counting on this job to come through. It could turn things around for us. We've still got a long way to go to get the company back on solid ground."

Exhaling a heavy breath, Gil ran a hand down the back of his neck. The recent setbacks at the company had forced his brother to make some tough decisions and a major sacrifice. "I should have been here. I let you down."

Linc held up his hand. "Stop. No one blames you. Abby was your first priority."

Mounting pressure in his chest drove Gil to his feet. "I let her down, too." His gaze came to rest on the family photo on the desk. "And Mom and Dad. Everyone."

"How do you figure?"

Gil brushed back his sport coat, setting his hands on his hips and keeping his back to his brother, his gaze fixed out the window. "I robbed Dad and Mom of their only grandchild. I promised Dad I'd bring her back home."

"And you did."

"Too late for him."

"Hey, at least you tried. Leah is the one who left and took Abby away."

"I should have fought harder. I should never have let Abby go with her mother in the first place. If I'd understood her illness better, I would never have allowed her full custody of Abby."

"We all believed that a toddler should be with her mother. None of us realized Leah was bipolar."

"But *I* should have. I was married to her. How stupid was I? I should have realized. The violent mood swings, the constant demand for more attention, the fact nothing was ever good enough. I thought she was spoiled. The worst part is she lied to me. If I hadn't stumbled on her meds when I went to pick up Abby that time, I'd never have known. Her sister, Pam, was only too eager to fill me in on how cruel I'd been."

"That's not true."

"Isn't it? If I'd known sooner, I could have helped her, gotten her better care, treated her differently. I might have been able to fix things."

"Gil, bipolar disorder isn't something you can fix. You know that. You're a smart guy."

"If I'm so smart, why didn't I see that my own wife was ill?"

"A better question would be, why didn't she tell you?"

The phone rang and Linc picked it up. Gil was only vaguely aware of the conversation. His brother's question was the same one he'd asked himself a million times. Why had Leah hidden her illness from him? Keeping him in the dark had only complicated all their lives and led to a string of bad decisions on his part. Regrets nagged at him constantly. He longed for the wise council of his father and the keen insight of his mother, neither of whom were available. He was on his own, free to make a whole new string of poor decisions with his daughter.

"That was a reminder that the bid on the Bancroft project is due this Friday."

"I'll have it ready." He glanced over his shoulder at his older brother. There were only thirteen months between them. They'd grown up more like twins. They could read each other's thoughts. Right now worry was written all over Linc's face. "I owe you an apology for fouling things up here." He rubbed his forehead, trying to ease the throbbing behind his eyes. "I left you to deal with everything after Dad died. I wasn't here to help with Mom or the company. I didn't take enough time on the bids."

"Gil, we all understood. The mess here with the company was all on me. I wasn't prepared to run the business. I never appreciated how good Dad was at running things here until he was gone."

"Me either. Do you think we can keep the place going?"

"I hope so. The family is depending on us."

Linc came from behind the desk and placed a hand on Gil's shoulder, giving it a brotherly squeeze. "You know, if you need to talk, I'm here."

"I know. I'd better get back. I'll be here early tomorrow. The nanny will be taking Abby to school from now on."

Linc nodded and patted his shoulder. "See you then. Oh, Mom said Beth came through the surgery on her tendon fine."

"Good to hear." Gil glanced at the photo again. Everyone in his family was suffering in some way. Without their father to serve as their anchor, they were all adrift.

The house was quiet when Gil stepped inside a short while later. The nanny was sitting at the kitchen table working on her tablet. She looked at him and smiled, bringing a glint into her brown eyes and revealing a dimple on one side of her mouth he hadn't noticed before. She had an infectious smile, wide and bright, that lit up the room. It almost made him want to smile back. He didn't. "Where's Abby? Is everything okay?"

"Yes, of course. She's in her room."

Gil tapped the tabletop with his fingers, fighting a fresh wave of concern. "Has she been there the whole time?"

"No. We had a snack, she showed me around the house and then she took me to her room. Did you know she doesn't like the color pink? Purple is her favorite."

He studied the woman. How did she know that? "No. She never said. I thought all girls like pink. My sisters did."

The nanny grinned as if placating a small child. "I think she'd like it if you could paint her room purple. Maybe she could help pick out the color."

He turned away, gathering himself as he slipped out of his sport coat. "Sure. We can do that." He took a seat at the table, clasping his hands. "I didn't have much time to get that room ready, and I never thought to ask about the color." Another misstep as a father. He should have asked Abby what she wanted, but it had never occurred to him. Once he'd been assured he would have full custody of his daughter, he'd hired one of the guys at the shop to paint the room and get it ready.

"Picking out things she likes will help her feel more at home. Change can be frightening for a child."

Resentment clogged Gil's throat. "Are you saying I frighten her?"

"No." She pressed her lips together. "But she thinks you don't want her here."

"She told you that?" His chest tightened.

"Yes. We talked a little and—"

"She *talked* to you?"

"Yes. Why?"

Gil stood, fighting the anger and hurt coursing through him. Abby hadn't said more than three words at a time to him since he'd brought her home, and those were usually clipped sentences. His mother had been able to coax some conversation from her, but not much. Yet this woman had learned more about his child in an hour than he had in weeks. He faced the nanny, her big brown eyes filled with puzzlement. "Abby doesn't talk much."

"She's struggling to adjust to her new life with you. She's lost her mother, been taken from everything familiar and put in a new situation. Spending one-on-one time with her, learning what she likes to do, will ease that transition. I've found that listening closely to the things they say can be very helpful."

"You think?" Was she accusing him of being a poor father? He'd heard that too often from his wife. He didn't need to it hear from an employee. "I think I know what's best for my daughter."

"Of course. I didn't mean to imply you didn't." She lowered her eyes, a faint blush staining her cheeks.

Gil squared his shoulders. This woman had no idea what he was going through. "Abby needs time, that's all."

"I'm sure you're right."

Now she was placating him. "Miss Bishop, I know you mean well, but I'd appreciate it if you'd remember that you are only here to care for my daughter until my mother returns."

"Yes, of course. I understand."

He tried to ignore the hurt look in her pretty brown eyes. He had a sinking sensation in his gut like he'd just kicked a sweet fuzzy bunny. He made a mental note to avoid eye contact with the attractive nanny. "Abby is fragile right now. I don't want her upset in any way. Just watch over her and let her have whatever she wants." He thought he saw a glint of disapproval in her eyes but shrugged it off. She couldn't possibly understand his situation. No one could.

Miss Bishop shut off her tablet and slipped it into her large bag. She stood and picked up a paper from the folder she'd been studying. She took a deep breath, as if preparing to deliver another blow. She held out the paper, and Gil braced himself.

"We drew pictures. It's a good way to find out what a child is thinking or feeling. This is what she drew."

Great. He could just imagine what she'd drawn. An ugly monster or maybe a man with a mean face? After he took the paper, he puzzled at the image. "A dog?"

The nanny gave him a tender smile that warmed her eyes and put a glow in her cheeks. "Apparently she had one named Cookie, but he went away. I thought maybe you could tell me what happened. She obviously cared deeply for the little dog."

Gil rubbed his bottom lip. "No. I don't know about any pets she might have had." He stared at the nanny. The compassion in her chocolate-brown eyes connected with a part of him he'd thought long dead. Her concern was directed at him. She understood what he was going through. It had been a long time since a woman had offered him understanding. The nanny was not only kind and intuitive, but she truly cared for others. No wonder Abby had taken to her so easily. That knowledge should make him happy. It didn't. "Truth is, I don't know much about her life for the last three years."

"Is there a reason you didn't go to see her?"

This nanny was also too inquisitive for his liking. He met her concerned gaze head-on. "I went every other weekend."

She lowered her gaze, then stood and gathered up the rest of her belongings. "It's just a suggestion, but a puppy would give her something to love and hold on to and make her feel more secure here."

It was a good idea. One he should have thought of himself. If that's all it would take to make his child happy, he'd buy her a dozen puppies. But why didn't she feel secure with him? What was he not doing that made Abby think she wasn't wanted? And how had this young nanny been able to connect with her in such a short time? "I'll think about it."

Miss Bishop took the hint and moved toward the door.

"Would you like me to start tomorrow, Mr. Montgomery?"

He wanted to call up the agency and tell them to send someone better suited. But this woman had connected with Abby in only an hour. He couldn't dismiss that fact. But she also had him off balance. It had been a long time since he'd noticed a woman, and he couldn't stop from noticing her. She brought light and energy to the room. "Yes. Be here by seven. I need to get to the shop early. I'll notify the school about the change. And please, call me Gil."

"And I'm Julie. I'll see you in the morning."

Gil watched her walk to her car, her dark wavy hair bobbing with each step. Somehow, Julie Bishop had managed to tear down his daughter's resistance and put a dent in his own barriers. Maybe the Lord was listening after all. Now it was his turn to take a crack at it.

He took the stairs two at a time. Abby was curled up on her bed when Gil entered her room, the same way she'd been since he'd brought her home. The worn polka-dot backpack was close at her side. "I'm home." He sat on the edge of the bed. "The nanny will be back tomorrow. She liked you a lot. Did you like her?"

Abby thought about that a moment before nodding.

"Good. I like her, too. She's going to be taking you to school each morning."

"Are you going away?"

"No." He reached out and squeezed her hand. "I just have lots of work to do. But I'll be home every night. Promise." She looked skeptical. "Miss Bishop…"

"She said to call her Miss Julie." Abby corrected him with a deep frown.

"Right. Miss Julie said you might like to have a puppy." A light appeared in Abby's eyes, causing Gil to catch his breath.

Abby nodded. "Can I?"

"Absolutely." His little girl smiled at him, and he thought his chest was going to explode with joy. "I'll get you whatever dog you want, sweet pea. I love you very much." Abby stared at him a long moment. Did she believe him? She would. Because he'd tell her that every hour until she had no doubts left.

"What's a sweet pea?"

He laughed and stroked her soft brown hair. She didn't pull away this time. "It's a pretty little flower that your grandma likes to grow."

"Oh. That's okay, then."

Progress. And he had the new nanny to thank.

Chapter Three

Julie pulled into the Montgomerys' driveway Wednesday morning and stopped beside Gil's Tahoe. She'd arrived early today, a result of her sleepless night. Her dreams had been filled with an assortment of odd images. Light, dark, happy, sad, all underscored with a deep sense of frustration. Her assignment wasn't going as she'd envisioned. Seeing her baby girl again was what she'd ached for since the moment they'd taken her away. She'd been eager to spend time with her child, but Abby was more inclined to retreat to her room with her backpack. She'd tried everything over the past two days to draw her out, with little success. All she'd managed to discover was that she liked hot chocolate, sugar cookies and chicken nuggets. They'd watched her favorite movie, *Cinderella*, but she refused to talk about school, or her mother or much of anything. She retreated to her room until supper, then went right back. The only thing she'd ask about was when she was going to get her puppy.

Julie ached for her. If she could get her to talk, to open up a little, she might be able to find the path to help Gil and his daughter connect. It was clear they needed each other, and she had only a few days to accomplish that goal.

Gil answered the door when she knocked, a deep frown on his face. He was usually so together when she arrived. But today he clearly wasn't ready. His hair was damp and uncombed. His face was slightly red from shaving, and the strong scent of his freshly applied aftershave wafted through her senses. The disheveled look worked for him. Abby's father was a very attractive man, with high cheekbones and a jawline cut from granite. But he was a man with a burden.

"Good. You're here. We're running late. I could use your help with Abby."

She followed him down the hall to the kitchen, keenly aware of his masculine appeal. Julie shut down that train of thought the moment she stepped into the kitchen. Abby was huddled over her cereal bowl. "Good morning, Abby." The little girl muttered a soft reply and waved her fingers.

Gil disappeared into the family room, returning a few moments later, looking more like the man she usually saw in the morning; his cotton button-up shirt now neatly tucked into the dark twill slacks, and his hair tamed.

"I have a conference call this morning. If you could help Abby get ready for school…"

"Of course."

He said goodbye to his daughter, placed a kiss on the top of her head then shrugged into his corduroy sport coat. Julie walked with him to the back door. "Have a good day." She smiled, her eyes locking with his. He stared back at her in surprise, as if no one had ever said those words to him before. Odd. Didn't everyone say that?

"You, too."

Moving to the counter, she poured a cup of coffee, studying her charge across the rim. She was such a lovely child. This morning her brown, sleep-tangled hair fell around her soft cheeks. When she finished her cereal, Julie placed the empty bowl on the counter. "Would you like me to fix your hair today? We could pull some of it over to one side so it wouldn't be falling in your eyes all the time." Abby nodded.

Julie followed her upstairs to the bathroom and picked up the brush, gently pulling it through the soft strands, then gathering the top section in a clump and fastening it with a small rubber band. Resting her hands on Abby's shoulders, she looked at their reflection in the mirror. "How do you like that?"

Abby nodded, a small smile on her lips, then she met Julie's gaze in the mirror and Julie's heart stopped. Her lungs seized. Abby looked exactly like her. The texture of her hair, her cheeks, her wide brown eyes and her narrow chin. Abby was a miniature version of her. It was so obvious Julie wondered why Gil Montgomery hadn't realized immediately who she was. What would she do now? Her throat squeezed shut. How could she stay here when it would be obvious to everyone that she was Abby's mother?

She sucked in a breath, causing Abby to turn and look at her. "We'd better get a move on. Don't want to be late for school."

Julie focused all her attention the rest of the day on her online students and the upcoming move to France. A long talk with DiDi had convinced her that she was overthinking the situation. Lots of people had brown hair and brown eyes. Besides, if Gil hadn't noticed yet, then he probably wouldn't. She would see him for only a few minutes in the morning and evening. She'd make a point to leave quickly when he came home. It was only for a few more days, and she wasn't ready to give up this time with Abby. Selfish but there it was.

By the time she picked Abby up from school, she was feeling confident again. Enough to attempt a small outing. Maybe putting her into a new environment, where she couldn't hide in her room, would encourage her to open up. "It's really chilly today. I thought we might go to that coffee shop downtown and get some hot chocolate. How does that sound?" Abby shrugged. "They serve cookies, too."

The Square Cup coffee shop on the town square was more charming than the pictures on its website. Tucked into a corner where two buildings intersected, the shop sported a red-and-white-striped awning over a sheltered outdoor eating area. Planters filled with pansies welcomed customers. Julie regretted she wouldn't be around in the warm weather to enjoy the spot.

A rush of warm air welcomed them in from the cold, wrapping them in the aroma of coffee and pastries. After placing their order at the counter, Julie steered Abby toward a table in the corner with a measure of privacy. Abby clutched her backpack on her lap, her gaze directed out the window. Julie couldn't blame her. Dover was a picturesque nineteenth-century town, with the courthouse as the centerpiece, surrounded by a park and ringed with charming brick stores on all sides. She longed to wander past the shops and explore the merchandise, but there wouldn't be time enough for that.

When their order arrived, Abby immediately started scooping out the marshmallows, eating them one at a time as she studied Julie's bag.

"Why do you have such a big purse?"

Julie smiled. Conversation at last. "My friend gave me this for my birthday, so it's special and I have a lot of important things I keep with me." She pointed to the backpack in Abby's lap. "Why do you carry that with you everywhere?"

Abby rubbed the top of the canvas bag. "It has my treasures in it. Mommy got it for me before she got sick."

She nodded. Now she understood. It was her last contact with her mother. "Treasures are important. So is schoolwork. Do you have any homework to do?" Abby dropped her chin to her chest, hugging the backpack, a sure sign she was avoiding something unpleasant. "Abby?"

Slowly she unzipped the bag and drew out a red folder with a label on which her name was printed. Abby's bottom lip pushed out.

For a brief second Julie hesitated to open the folder. She suspected there was either a bad grade or a parent note. Gil should be the one to address the issue, but Abby had given it to her. She opened the folder and found a note from her teacher, Mrs. Taylor, attached to the first page, expressing her concern that Abby was not interacting with the other students and not participating in classroom activities. She requested a conference as soon as possible.

The observation came as no surprise to Julie. She'd dealt with similar issues with some of her students. Moving to a new town, a divorce or death in the family often sent children into withdrawal. She grinned at Abby, hoping to ease her fears. "Would you like me to give this to your father when he comes home or would you like to do it?"

"You."

Her whispered reply was barely audible.

"Abby? Abby Montgomery? Hello, darling."

Julie glanced up at the middle-aged woman with the friendly smile approaching the table. "I'm Nancy Scott, your neighbor. Remember, I brought you and your daddy brownies last week?" She pointed at Julie. "And you must be the nanny. Francie hated that she had to leave Abby just when they got her back, but she had go to England to be with Bethany."

Mentally, she sorted out the information. Francie would be Gil's mother, and Bethany probably the sister who danced. "Julie Bishop. I'll be filling in until her grandmother gets back." She had the impression the woman wouldn't leave without at least a brief conversation. "Won't you join us?"

"Well, just for a moment. Nice to meet you, Julie. I'm in the brick house right next door. If you need anything or you want some company, don't hesitate to drop by. My husband and I own the jewelry store catty-corner from here. Scott's Fine Jewelry. We've been friends with the Montgomerys for years. So sad about Dale's passing. Gil's father. Happened this past September. Such a shock."

"I didn't know." Losing his father might explain some of Gil's dark mood. Losing his father and his former wife would be painful.

"That's a lovely necklace you have on."

Julie touched the silver heart, willing herself not to

look at Abby. "Thank you." Noticing a stack of papers in Mrs. Scott's hands, she steered the conversation in that direction to avoid further discussion on the necklace. "Are you handing out fliers?"

"Yes, I am." She handed one to Julie. "It's for the annual Father-Daughter Night at Peace Community Church. I'm the chairperson this year." She looked at Abby. "You'll have to ask your daddy to take you. There's a lovely dinner and a talent show. I know you'd enjoy spending an evening with your daddy, wouldn't you?"

Julie noticed Abby's confused look and diverted Mrs. Scott's attention again. "Talent show. That's a big job. I coordinated our school talent show for a few years."

Nancy inhaled, laying her hand on Julie's. "You did? I could certainly use your expertise on this event."

"Oh, that's very nice, but I'm only in Dover for the week."

"What a shame. Well, I'd better get back to work. Lots of fliers to hand out. Nice to meet you, Julie. 'Bye, Abby. I'll see you again real soon."

Julie's smile quickly slid into a grimace of astonishment when the woman disappeared from sight. "She sure likes to talk, doesn't she?" Abby's eyes brightened in understanding, and she nodded before taking another sip of her cocoa.

On the ride home, Julie tried to get more information from Abby about her class and the other kids, but she barely responded. With no homework, she went directly to her room and closed the door. Julie placed the note in the center of the breakfast room table. She'd make sure to give it to Gil the moment he came home.

In fact it might be a good idea to have a conversation with him about his daughter. If she was going to help Abby overcome her insecurities, she needed to know what she'd been— Julie put her hands on her cheeks. She had to stop that train of thought. She had to remember this was temporary. Like Cinderella at the ball, the clock would strike soon and it would all end. No one could ever know who she was. Ever.

Gil pulled his SUV into the drive Thursday evening and shut off the engine. He managed to get home early tonight. In the three days since Julie Bishop had been working for him, he'd had to stay at the office until late, and he hadn't had a chance to talk with her at length about Abby since she'd given him the note from Mrs. Taylor. Julie had wanted to discuss it with him right then, but he'd blown her off. He didn't need any outside help. Julie had taken it upon herself that second night to prepare supper, and the welcoming aromas had triggered memories and old dreams he'd long buried. A warm meal, a woman waiting, his child happy to see him. Knowing it could never be had soured his mood. Thankfully Julie never stayed to eat with them, claiming the early darkness of winter made her eager to make the long drive back to Jackson before it got too late.

He'd met with Mrs. Taylor this afternoon and wasn't happy with her comments. The teacher was concerned about Abby's shyness, the chip on her shoulder and her overdependence on her backpack.

If only his dad were here, or his mom. He could go to them about anything, only now he'd have to figure it out on his own. He knew he should talk to Julie about the situation, but the idea rubbed him the wrong way.

Knowing that his child had been reluctant to give him the note, and had given it to Julie instead, left a heavy weight on his mind. Was she afraid he'd send her away?

Girlish giggles greeted him the moment he opened the kitchen door. He stopped, stunned at the sound. The soft laughter was from the nanny. The giggles? He moved into the room, his gaze searching out his daughter. She was up on her knees in a kitchen chair, leaning over a board game in the center of the table. He stared at the pair. Abby turned over a card and squealed. "Sorry. Sorry. You have to go back."

The nanny made a great show of disappointment, laughing and moving her game piece slowly around the board.

His heart contracted. Abby was laughing. He'd thought he'd never hear that from her. "What's going on here?"

Abby jerked her head in his direction, a smile lighting her face. "Hi, Daddy. I'm winning."

Gil couldn't speak around the lump in his throat. Instead he walked to his daughter and rested his hand on her head, staring at her sweet happy face. "You are? That's great. What are you playing?"

"Sorry. Miss Julie taught me." He looked over at Julie. Her hands were clasped in front of her mouth and moisture glistened in her eyes. His temporary nanny had a soft heart for those in her care. He started to ask her what she'd done to cause Abby to laugh, but the front doorbell chimed.

Julie stood and reached for her purse, glancing over her shoulder at him. "Pizza delivery. Abby, can you put the game away, please?"

Abby looked up at him. "We're having pizza. You want some?"

He brushed a few strands of hair off her cheek and tucked it behind her ear. "Sure. That sounds nice. So you and Miss Julie had fun today?" Abby nodded. "Your grandma and your new cousin, Evan, like to play this game. Now you can play with them."

Gil helped place the lid on the game box and set it aside. When he looked back up, Julie was placing the pizza box in the center of the table. The aroma made his stomach growl.

"I hope you like everything on your pizza."

"I do. Is there something I can do to help?"

"Drinks? Abby, sweetie, will you get the plates and napkins?"

He watched in amazement as Abby happily did as she was asked. He'd deliberately not asked much of her, believing she needed the freedom to adjust, but maybe leaving her to do as she pleased wasn't the best way either. His mood sagged. He should know that. He was her father. But this young teacher was far more adept at caring for his child than he was.

Julie fit easily into their life. In the past few days he'd looked forward to seeing her when he came home, even if it was only a brief encounter. She was always smiling and upbeat. No wonder Abby adored her. She would be an easy woman to love. Julie turned and caught him staring.

"Is something wrong?"

He cleared his throat and shut down his wayward thoughts. "No. I could never get her to help with anything. She always sulked and went to her room."

Julie smiled, flashing her lone dimple. "I didn't give

her a choice. We all have to pitch in. I think she enjoys it now."

He got the hint. That's the way it had been in his family. Everyone did his or her part. No options available. But none of them had been through what Abby had. He didn't want to do anything to upset her or cause more distress.

Seated at the table, Gil let the peaceful feeling seep through him. Julie did most of the talking, telling him what she and Abby had done in the afternoon, how Abby had won the most games of Sorry and some of the funny things her online students wrote in their papers.

"When are we going to get my puppy?"

He'd been enjoying the meal so much he'd forgotten about the weekend plans. "Saturday morning. Your uncle Linc and I are taking you and Evan to the shelter in Sawyer's Bend so you can pick out your pets." The big smile and bright eyes on his child's face stole his breath. If only he could make her this happy every second of her life.

Julie chuckled softly. "Have you thought about a name for your dog?"

"Not yet. But I'll know after I pick it out."

After cleaning up the kitchen, Julie sent Abby upstairs to get ready for bed.

Gil called after her as she left the room. "I'll be up to tuck you in, sweet pea."

"I want Julie to do it," Abby said.

All the blood drained from his face. Of course she did. "Good night, then. Sleep tight."

He glanced over at Julie. The tenderness in her eyes drew him. "No Father-of-the-Year awards for me."

"Be patient. It'll take time. She's gotten used to me, and she hasn't seen much of you this week."

His defenses kicked in. "I couldn't help it. Our business is on life support right now. We would have lost the company if my brother hadn't stepped in. I need to be there."

"That wasn't a reprimand. I'm just pointing out she's spent more time with me, that's all. But I have a suggestion." She pulled a sheet of paper from the counter. "Your church is holding a father-daughter dinner soon. You could take Abby. It would be a special outing for you both. I think she'd like that."

Gil studied the paper. What would they talk about over dinner? "I'm not so sure, but I'll think about it." He could tell she wasn't pleased with his response, but he had more important things on his mind.

She tilted her head, a half smile causing her dimple to briefly appear. "How did the meeting with Mrs. Taylor go?"

He rubbed his temple. Another sore spot. It had been a lousy day—except for coming home and hearing Abby's laughter. "She seems to think I should force Abby to participate in school and make friends."

"Is that really what she said? I'm a teacher, and we only send notes like the one she sent when we have concerns for the student's well-being."

"How can she know what's best for Abby after only a few weeks?"

"Experience."

"Seems to me she's just putting more pressure on her." Gil glanced up when Abby called for Julie from upstairs.

"I'll be right back. But you should go and say good-night, too. Later."

"She doesn't want me." Julie caught him off guard when she rested her small hand on his arm. The warmth of her touch soothed his disappointment.

"Go anyway."

Gil retreated to the office, hoping to sort through his emotional turmoil. In a short span of time he'd gone from irritation to joy to hurt. He'd never anticipated the hostility and rejection from his daughter. Or that she would latch on to a stranger. Clearly Julie had an ability with children he lacked. Yet every inroad she made left him feeling resentful. He needed advice. Direction. Things his parents had always provided, but Dad was gone and Mom was out of the country. He glanced at the clock. Not a good time to call his mother. Not a good time for much of anything.

Julie tucked Abby in and said good-night, telling her that her father would be up to see her soon, gently reminding her how much he loved her. The kitchen was empty when she returned, so she went in search of her employer and found him in the office off the family room. She'd never been inside. The door was usually closed, but not this evening. The room was predictably masculine with a dark wooden desk and brown leather chair. There was a drafting board set to one side, where a round container held rolls of blueprints.

But it was Gil who drew her attention. He stood in front of the fireplace, his hands clutching the mantel edge as he stared into the firebox. The dejected slope of his broad shoulders said it all. Abby had hurt him deeply with her comments. Her heart went out to him.

He wanted desperately to connect with his child, but he was floundering.

"Abby is all tucked in. I told her you'd be up to say good-night later."

Gil straightened and faced her, shoving his hands into his pockets. He pressed his lips together. "She doesn't want to see me."

Julie's heart ached. She didn't know whom she wanted to comfort more, Abby or her dad. "That's not true. She does, she's just confused and uncertain. If you don't mind me asking, is there more going on with Abby than losing her mother?"

He stared at the floor a long moment before answering. When he met her gaze again, she saw sparks of anger flash in his blue eyes. "Remember when you asked me why I didn't see Abby after the divorce? It's because my wife lied to me."

Julie's conscience pricked.

"She was bipolar, but she never bothered to share that fact with me and I was too blind to put it all together. I didn't find out about her illness until a year after the divorce. I found her meds and confronted her. She accused me of spying on her. That's when I started trying to regain custody of Abby. I didn't know anything about bipolar disorder. There'd been nothing like that in my family. Do you have any idea how it affects people?"

"I do. My close friend's mother is bipolar."

"Then you know the damage it can do to children."

Wrapping her arms around her middle, she tried to fend off the images of what little Abby might have endured and keep her focus on Gil. "I do."

"I started custody proceedings, but that only made

Leah angrier. That's when she and her sister started their campaign to discredit me. Every time I showed up in Mobile to visit Abby for the weekend, there was some new hoop to jump through or some event that had come up that demanded Abby stay with them. One time I'd gotten as far as Hattiesburg when the police stopped me and said I had no right to take Abby across state lines."

Julie moved closer. "Oh, Gil, I'm so sorry. That must have been horrible for you."

He ran a hand along his jaw. "I can only guess what they told Abby about me. She probably thinks I'm some kind of monster."

"I don't think she does. But you will have to work harder to show her how much you love her. Find out what movies she likes to watch. Read to her each night. Tell her about yourself, and share the memories you have from when she was a baby. And don't let her retreat to her room so much." She crossed her arms over her chest. "Has Abby been to see a psychologist about her grief?"

"Yes. And he said she's shy and she'll come out of it when she's ready, and not to push her."

"I don't agree."

Gil narrowed his gaze. "What makes you an expert? Do you have children?"

Julie blanched. "No. But I do have a degree in child psychology and years of experience with children."

"But that doesn't give you the right to…"

His cell ringtone intruded. He pulled it from his pocket and stepped away. When he faced her again, she could see the deep concern in his eyes and the hard set of his jaw.

"Is everything all right?"

"No. More bad news. We lost a bid we were counting on."

"Sorry."

He pinched the bridge of his nose. "Forget what I said earlier. I appreciate all you've done. I just want to make her laugh the way you did. How did you do that?"

The pleading in his eyes drew her closer. She looked up at him, her gaze skimming the faint stubble appearing on his face and the small scar beneath his lower lip. She wondered where he'd gotten it. "Time together. We talk on the way to and from school. We are together each afternoon until you come home. She's gotten comfortable with me."

"You make it sound so easy."

"And you're making it much too hard."

She rested her hand on his forearm, sending a charge through her system that fired every nerve ending to life. She pulled her hand away. Something about Gil compelled her to draw closer, to know him better. That was something she couldn't afford. Especially after learning his wife lied to him. "Relax, Gil. Love her. That's all that matters. It's late. I need to go."

He followed her to the door. She looked up at him, resisting the impulse to reach up and caress his cheek to ease his worry. "Go up and say good-night to your daughter. She's expecting you."

Julie fought tears all the way home. She cried for Gil, who was longing for his child's love, for Abby and the chaotic life she must have lived with her mother and for herself, for bringing another lie into the Montgomerys' life. What a mess this was. Thankfully, tomorrow was her last day. She'd have to pray that Gil's mother could guide the pair to a new relationship. But in her heart, she knew she was the only one who could do that. She had a bond with Abby neither of them had.

Biology.

Julie waved goodbye to Abby, then pulled away from the school, unable to shake the shroud of sadness dampening her spirits. Today was her last day as nanny, and she was determined to embrace every moment, imprint each second in her heart and mind. They'd have to last for the rest of her life. But how would she ever find the strength to walk away from sweet Abby?

Stepping into the Montgomery kitchen a short while later, she allowed her gaze to travel around the room. Memories flowed through her. How had she become so entangled in such a short amount of time? Her lungs squeezed painfully in her chest. She wasn't ready to walk away from Abby. Or Gil. He was a good man who loved his daughter dearly. She'd found several books around the house on parenting, which told her he was committed to helping his child. But he was afraid of making mistakes and instead was too lenient.

Opening her laptop, she attempted to work, but her mind kept drifting into dangerous territory. What would her life have been like if she'd chosen to keep her little girl? In her fantasies she saw herself nobly carrying on, working, going to school, all the while toting a baby on her hip. But the ugly truth slapped her in the face. Welfare. Food stamps. A one-room apartment. Shift work at a fast-food place or a quick-stop. A little girl with no hope. No toys. No future.

Turning on her cell phone, she opened it to her pictures. She'd taken as many of her little girl as she could and several of her father. She scrolled through them to the one she'd caught of him looking lovingly at his daughter. The tenderness in his cobalt eyes, the slight smile on his mouth, had lodged in her heart. She had many regrets about leaving, but one of the biggest was that she'd never seen Gil smile. She wanted to see him happy. She suspected Gil's smile would be a heart-stopping sight.

With a low groan, she closed the app. She was only making things worse. By the time she went to pick up Abby, her nerves were frayed and a lead weight lay in the pit of her stomach. She was determined to ignore the physical distress and have as much quality time with Abby as she could squeeze in to these last few hours.

She was preparing a small snack of apple slices when Abby came to her side to watch. "Almost ready. Do you want to sit at the table or in the family room?"

"Miss Julie, I like you."

Julie's heart melted, tears stung the backs of her eyes. Unable to stop herself, she pulled the child into her arms and held her close. "Oh, Abby, I like you, too." It was the first time she'd hugged her, and now she didn't think she could ever let her go. *But she's not my child.* Julie ended the embrace and stepped back.

Tears welled up in Abby's eyes. "I wish you could stay longer."

"I do, too, but your dad only needed my help for a few days. Your grandma should be back soon to take care of you. You'll like that."

"I guess."

She hugged her close. "I couldn't stay much longer

anyway. Remember, I told you I'm moving to France soon to teach in a school." After learning how Abby felt everyone in her life went away, Julie had explained about her job overseas. Abby hadn't made a fuss. But that was when they were still getting to know one another. She hoped her departure now wouldn't be too upsetting.

Julie tried to keep the mood light the rest of the day, but Abby grew more and more quiet after dinner, which only increased her own guilt. Five days with her daughter had given her the reassurance she'd craved, but the interaction may have had the opposite effect on Abby. It was good that her assignment was over today.

Gil had worked late again, so they'd eaten without him. Abby retreated to her room immediately after. Julie had tried to coax her into watching a movie, but she'd refused.

Julie met him at the back door when he got home. Her expression must have revealed her tension because he searched her face, a frown drawing his dark brows together. "I saved you some supper. It's in the oven."

"Thanks." He glanced around the kitchen. "Where's Abby?"

"She's in her room. She's not happy about me leaving."

Gil shrugged out of his sport coat and rubbed his bottom lip. "Yeah, I want to talk to you about that. Something has come up. Mom is staying in London longer than she expected. At least four more weeks, so I'm going to need help with Abby. I'd like you to stay on."

Her mind balked at the idea. Four weeks? Impossible. She'd be a fool to risk exposure, not to mention the threat to her own mental stability with such a long-term stay. Dread pooled in the center of her chest. And what was she going to do now?

She couldn't do this. If she was having trouble leaving her child after five days, how could she ever let her go after a month? But what if, by staying those extra weeks, she could unite father and daughter the way they were supposed to be? Then she could leave for Paris without any regrets or doubts.

She turned away, unable to look at the hope in Gil's eyes. No. It was out of the question. It was completely wrong. Fighting the urge to grab her belongings and run from the house, she struggled to remain calm. This was her chance to back out. She'd found what she'd come for. Abby would be happy in time. Gil would see to it. She met his eyes and opened her mouth. "Of course. I'd be happy to stay on."

Relief was clearly written on his face, and the corner of his mouth lifted. "Which brings up something else I've been meaning to discuss. I'd like you to consider moving into the apartment above the garage. That way you'll be available to watch Abby on short notice."

"I don't know."

"I mentioned our business is facing some problems. The truth is we're struggling to survive. There are a few out-of-town projects that I might have to check on, which would require an overnight stay. Linc usually handles that part of a job, but he's planning his wedding and I need to carry my share of the load. He's been doing it for too long."

Julie clasped her fingers together. It was logical, practical and dangerous. She'd never anticipated this. But the opportunity to have more time with her little girl—and with Gil—was too tempting to pass up. "I suppose that would be more convenient for all of us."

"Good. You can move in tomorrow. Linc and I are taking Abby and Evan to pick out their dogs. The apartment is completely furnished down to the dishes, so all you'll need is your personal belongings." He pulled a key from the drawer and handed it to her. "I appreciate this, Julie. You've helped my little girl. I didn't think I'd ever see her smile again."

His sincere tone touched her. "She's a special child. All she needs is love."

"She has all I can give her. Always."

Julie fingered the key. There was no turning back now. She was as deeply embedded in the Montgomerys' life as she could get. The only thing she could do was make it her mission to bring Abby and her dad together. Then she'd step aside. It would make it harder on her, but that's what she deserved for thinking this situation was a good idea.

All she could do now was to try to right the wrong before she had to walk away from them forever.

Chapter Four

Friday night was girls' night for Julie and DiDi. It had been for years. The only time they missed was when Julie lived in Huntsville, Alabama, for a year, and the two weeks Di and her husband, Ed, were on their honeymoon. But tonight Julie wasn't looking forward to getting together. She'd been dreading telling her friend about the change in plans with the Montgomerys. She poured tea into the glasses, painfully aware of her friend's disapproving glare on her back.

"What are you thinking? You can't stay on as the nanny for a month. It's too risky. Please tell me you're kidding."

Julie handed the glass to her friend, then took a seat at the small kitchen table in her duplex. "I couldn't say no. Abby and I have finally connected. She's starting to smile." Julie pulled up the photo of Abby she'd taken yesterday and slid the cell across the table. "She's beautiful, Di." DiDi picked up the phone, but instead of the smile she expected, DiDi's dark eyes grew wide in surprise.

"Julie, you cannot stay on this job." She turned the

phone around to show her the image on the screen. "She looks exactly like you. Anyone who sees you together will know you're her mother."

She took the phone back and closed the picture. "You're the one who said lots of people have brown hair and brown eyes."

"That's before I saw her."

Julie bit down hard on her lip and shook her head. "I can't leave right now. Abby needs me. With a little more time I can help her and her father have the relationship they deserve."

"That's not your job, Julie." DiDi stared at her a long moment. "Sometimes I wish I'd never given you the parents' names. I think I made it all worse." She reached over and squeezed Julie's arm. "I just wanted to help. You were so sad and alone. I thought if I found out who adopted her, it would give you some comfort."

"It did. But nothing can change what I did."

"You had no choice. If only your parents…"

Julie abruptly stood and pointed to her friend's nearly empty glass. "More tea?"

Di pursed her lips together. "Sure. Look, Julie. You have to deal with them someday."

It was an old argument. One with no solution. Her parents had turned their backs on her the day of her sister's accident. From that moment on, they'd offered no moral support, no financial support, no compassion of any kind. She'd been on her own.

Her conscience quickly reminded her that she wasn't being completely honest. She'd told that story for so long she'd started to believe it. The truth was, life for the Bishops had changed after her sister, a competitive diver, had suffered an accident that left her a quadriplegic. Caring for Maryann had consumed all her parents' time, energy and money. The strain had destroyed the family. Her father had become bitter and angry. Her mother, burdened with the full-time care of her oldest daughter, had been drained of all joy and hope. It was no one's fault, but Julie had been shoved aside, ignored. When Julie had found out she was pregnant, she'd told Di that her parents wouldn't help. It had been simpler than trying to explain the real reason. The truth was her parents never knew because she'd never told them. They'd had enough to deal with caring for her sister. One more burden would have destroyed them all. Going it alone had been the better option.

DiDi exhaled an exasperated sigh. "I should have seen this coming. You get all caught up in helping your kids and next thing you know you're emotionally involved and then your heart is broken and theirs is, too."

She opened her mouth to protest, but the truth of her friend's statement couldn't be dismissed. Di shifted to look directly at her. "Julie, you shouldn't even be wondering about her problems, let alone trying to fix them."

Guilt rolled up into her chest. "I know but—"

Di waved off her comment. "There are no *buts* in this situation. You said you only wanted to make sure she was happy, with a family that loved her. You've done that. Now let it go."

"But…"

"Julie, you always give your whole heart to those in your care. How can you not give it to your own child? But she's not yours."

Di was right. Abby didn't belong to her. She was Gil Montgomery's child. But she'd already made the commitment. She'd have to be careful, keep her heart locked up tight.

DiDi reached over and took her hand.

"Do you remember last year when I thought Ed was having an affair?"

Julie remembered how helpless she'd felt. "Yes. He'd lost his job, and he didn't know how to tell you."

"Right, but the point is, keeping the truth from me nearly destroyed our marriage. Secrets are like cancer to relationships. They eat away from the inside. Be careful how you handle this situation. It could hurt a lot of people."

DiDi's warning was clear. She was keeping a huge secret from the Montgomerys. One that could shatter all their lives. But telling the truth posed an even bigger danger. All she could do for now was be cautious and vigilant. She had no choice.

Saturday morning welcomed a span of warm weather for late January. Today's highs would be in the low seventies, making it a good day to move into the garage apartment. Pulling into the Montgomerys' driveway, Julie tried to be as quiet as possible, not wanting to disturb Abby and Gil. But as she set her large suitcase onto the ground, the back door opened and Gil stepped out.

"I hadn't expected you so soon."

"I'm sorry if I woke you."

"No. You warned me you were an early riser."

Julie shrugged. "I figured I'd spend the day getting settled in."

Gil pulled up the handle on her suitcase. "If you'll give me the key I'll help you carry your things up."

"Thank you." Julie pulled the smaller case from the trunk and followed Gil to the outside steps along the side of the garage that led to the apartment. He looked different today in a pair of worn and faded jeans that hugged his long legs and a long-sleeve T-shirt that fit snug across his broad shoulders. Stubble shadowed his jaw, and his wavy hair called attention to his intense blue eyes and softened the sharp angles of his face.

He carried her large case up the wooden stairs as if it weighed nothing. It would have taken her much longer, dragging the luggage up one step at a time. Inside, Gil rolled her suitcase into the room at the back she assumed was the bedroom as she surveyed the small apartment. The living room/kitchen combination was cozy and welcoming.

Gil stepped to the sink and turned it on. "I meant to check the place out before you got here to make sure the water and heat were working. Looks okay."

"I'm sure it'll be fine. This is charming."

He nodded. "The woman who sold me the house added the apartment for her granddaughter to live in while she was in college in Jackson."

More questions to add to her growing list about her child. "Abby didn't grow up here?"

"No. We had a home in Sawyer's Bend. I sold it. I bought this place last year."

That explained the odd mix of furniture and the disjointed appearance of their home.

"Julie, I really appreciate you agreeing to this arrangement. I'll feel better knowing you're close by."

"I'm happy to help. Besides, this apartment is nicer than my duplex at the moment." She hastened to explain. "I've been getting rid of most of my furniture and things. I won't be able to take much with me when I move overseas."

"How long will you be there?"

"Five years. Probably longer."

"That's a long time to be away from home." The word unleashed an unexpected twinge of homesickness. She hadn't had a real home in a long time. She'd had a place to live, but the sense of home had been missing since she'd left her parents. "Yes, it is, but it'll be an adventure, too." She grinned and quickly changed the subject. "Is Abby excited about going to the animal shelter?"

"Yes. I'm surprised she's not up already begging me to go pick up Linc and Evan." He looked at her for a moment, then glanced around. "Well, if there's anything else I can do, let me know."

"Thank you. I'm just going to take it easy, maybe stock up the pantry."

"Okay. There's a Piggly Wiggly a few blocks away and a large chain grocery by the school." Gil stopped at the door. "Abby is excited about you staying on. You have a special way with her. My mother has that ability, too. She connected with Abby right away. Thank you. It means a lot to me."

Tongue-tied at his unexpected compliment, she could only nod. When the door shut behind him, Julie moved to the bedroom. He'd placed her suitcase on the bed for easy access. Pulling the zipper, she opened the top, then stared down at her neatly folded clothing. Gil had praised her special way with Abby. He had no idea how special that bond actually was.

Her conscience flared. This was wrong. She knew she had to back out of this assignment before everyone got hurt. Most especially her child. Pivoting, she went to the living area and retrieved her cell phone, placing a call to Agatha from the nanny agency.

"Julie, dear. It's so good to hear from you. I'm so thankful you agreed to stay on there."

She chewed her bottom lip. "I need to talk to you about that."

"Of course, but first I want to tell you that Mr. Montgomery called here yesterday and praised your work. He said you were a blessing to his daughter. Julie, I wish I had ten more nannies like you. Especially now."

"Why now?"

"You know turnover here is always a challenge, but I've had three resignations this week alone and the applicants I'm getting aren't nearly as qualified as I'd like. I can't tell you what a blessing it is to know that I never have to worry about your assignments."

Julie leaned against the counter, hanging her head. How could she back out of this job now?

"So what did you want to talk about?"

"Nothing. I just wanted to let you know everything is going well." Agatha asked about her progress toward her big move and expressed her appreciation again. Her hope of escaping this job was dashed. With Agatha in a bind, she couldn't walk away. There was no choice for the time being but to forge ahead.

Gil glanced in his rearview mirror at his daughter sitting in the backseat. She'd been smiling since she'd bounced into the kitchen this morning. It was a good thing they'd planned to go to the animal shelter early because Abby was ready to burst with anticipation over getting a puppy.

"How much farther, Coach?"

Gil chuckled at Evan's question and his continued use of the title. Linc had been coaching Evan's flag football team, and Gil wondered how long it would be before he started calling Linc Dad.

"We're still in Dover, buddy. Hold your horses."

He shared a knowing smile with his brother. Linc had taken Evan to his heart as if he was his own son. It was good to see his brother so happy. Gemma, the woman he was going to marry in a few weeks, had brought joy and peace to his older brother. Something that had been missing for a long time.

Gil never entertained the idea of finding someone himself. After his disastrous marriage to Leah, he'd accepted that he wasn't good at relationships. He would be content to have his daughter back. That was a big enough blessing. He wouldn't ask for more. An image of Julie fluttered through his mind, her bright smile, her easy laughter, the way her warm brown eyes flashed with emotion. The way she thought of others first, even him. In one short week she'd brought a new energy and warmth into his home. If he could find someone like her to share his life with, he might rethink getting married again. He squelched the thought. His nanny was moving to France, and he wasn't about to risk another heartbreak.

By the time he pulled to a stop at the shelter in Sawyer's Bend, Evan and Abby were ready to jump from the car before he'd shut off the engine. After visiting with every dog in the building, Evan chose a friendly four-month-old German shepherd, and Abby settled on a small black mixed-breed pup with curly fur and floppy ears.

It wasn't until they'd dropped Linc and Evan off at home that Gil realized he'd omitted a vital piece from the get-Abby-a-dog equation. Linc's fiancée, Gemma, had already purchased food, bowls, a dog bed and all the other necessary pet supplies. Abby was adamant that they show off the new puppy, dubbed Ruffles, to Julie and bring her along to the pet store. She hopped out of the car and started up the apartment stairs before he could stop her.

Julie stepped out onto the landing and looked down at him. Abby took her hand and hurried her down to the car.

"She's black with curly hair and floppy ears," Abby said breathlessly. Gil raised the lift gate so Julie could get a closer look at the new puppy.

Abby stuck her hands through the cage and touched the little dog. Another item Gil had overlooked. Thankfully the shelter offered them for sale.

"She's adorable." Julie met his gaze, her dark eyes glinted with delight, bringing a soft pink tinge into her cheeks. The word *adorable* could apply to her, as well. Her gaze told him she approved of his decision, and it unleashed a warmth along his nerve endings. Though why he should want to please the nanny was unclear.

"I'm afraid I didn't think this puppy thing through. We have no food, no bed, nothing."

"Please come with us to pick out Ruffles's bed and toys." Abby clasped her hands together, begging her to come.

Julie looked at Gil, who shrugged. "I really could use your help. But this is your day off, so I'll understand if you can't."

"I'd love to shop for Ruffles. Let me get my purse and lock up."

Abby kept up a running conversation with her new puppy even though he was in the back and she fastened in the seat belt.

Gil glanced at the woman beside him. "Suggesting a dog was a great idea. She's already fallen in love with him. Look how happy she is."

"She is, isn't she? You would have figured it out on your own."

"I'm not so sure. Abby told you about her other dog. Not me." He hated the note of bitterness that crept into his tone.

"That'll change. The more time you spend together, the closer you'll become."

He doubted that, but he didn't want to argue. "I hope so. She's been with me weeks now, and I don't see much change." He stole a glance at Julie. He'd almost said "until you showed up."

An hour later and a few hundred dollars poorer, Gil was questioning the puppy idea. He and Julie were watching Abby play with Ruffles in the backyard. "You really think having a dog will make her feel better about being here. With me?"

"There's no magic formula, Gil. Nothing that will flip a switch and make Abby suddenly happy and contented. But yes, pets are wonderful therapy tools. Not just for children but soldiers, the elderly, the handicapped. I'm sure you'll be amazed at the difference that little puppy will make."

Abby brought the dog back inside, her face aglow. "Ruffles likes it here."

Gil nodded. "I'm sure she does. She has the most expensive dog paraphernalia in town."

"What's that?"

Julie giggled softly. "It means Ruffles has lots of nice things. Have you thought about where Ruffles is going to sleep?"

"With me."

Gil set his hands on his hips. "That's not going to happen. The lady at the shelter was very clear about crate training the dog. Once Ruffles is a little older and housebroken, then we'll see about her staying in your room."

"No. I want her with me all the time." Abby stuck her lower lip out.

"Sweet pea, she's still a puppy. I'll not have her leaving little surprises all over the house."

Abby burst into tears. "She needs me. She needs to be with me at night. She'll be scared all alone."

The tears and the whining were his undoing. Seeing his daughter so upset drilled into his core. She'd been through so much. The dog was the first thing she'd shown interest in since he'd brought her home. Maybe he was being too harsh. "Okay. We'll compromise. She can sleep in your room, but she has to stay in the crate. Is that clear?"

Abby scooped up Ruffles and hugged her until she squirmed. "Let's play with your new toys." She scurried off to the living room. Gil watched her go, his chest a twisted knot of doubt and hope. He turned back to find Julie watching him with a disapproving look. "What? You think I shouldn't have given in?"

"It's not for me to say. But that puppy will whine all night. It'll keep her awake and probably you, too."

He bristled at her statement. "You saw how upset she was. I just want to make her happy."

"Giving in to her every demand won't accomplish that."

"Neither will being the bad guy." A look of exasperation flitted across Julie's features, leaving a nugget of doubt in his mind. Maybe he should have put his foot down. But what would it hurt for Abby to have the dog in her room if it made her happy? Wasn't that the whole point of the pet thing?

"I'm sure you know what's best."

The tone of her voice suggested otherwise. She held his gaze a long moment, as if trying to send a message. He lifted his chin. He appreciated her concern, but he knew what was best for Abby. All he wanted to do was make her happy and protect her from disappointment or sadness.

She picked up her purse and started toward the door. "Thank you for including me today. It was fun. I'm sure Abby and Ruffles are going to be inseparable. I wanted to ask you what church you attend. I don't want to drive all the way back to Jackson tomorrow for services."

He was surprised by the question. Since the death of his father and then his ex-wife, his church attendance had dwindled along with his faith. His mother had been nudging him lately to bring Abby to church. He wasn't sure why he was dragging his feet. "Peace Community. My family has been members there for years. It's downtown, right off the square on the north side. The big red brick building with the white steeple."

"What time do services start?"

"I don't know. I haven't been there in a while. They

have a website." She gave him a questioning look. Clearly she was surprised with his response.

"I'll check it. Thank you."

From the back-door window, Gil watched Julie walk across the drive and up the steps to her apartment. The nanny had very firm ideas on how children should be handled, but she didn't understand his and Abby's unique situation. If he'd been able to raise his child, things would be different. But he was playing catch-up, trying to overcome years of separation, lies and constant meddling. It would take time. First he wanted to make Abby happy. Then they'd work through the other stuff. Such as overcoming his burning guilt for relinquishing full custody to her mother. He'd make it up to her if it was the last thing he ever did, if he could figure out how.

A wave of remorse surged through his heart and mind. He knew where to begin. He just wasn't comfortable with the idea. It was time to confront his mistakes. Tomorrow he and Abby would go to church. He'd been at odds with the Lord too long.

Sunday morning proved to be more difficult than he'd expected. Abby wasn't too happy about leaving Ruffles alone while they went to church. She'd sent a steady stream of nasty glares in his direction, but he'd held firm. She'd stomped around the house, refused to finish her breakfast and complained that she hated her dress.

He'd resorted to bribery, promising to take her to the big pet store in Sawyer's Bend to buy a new toy for Ruffles. His conscience told him that was a bad move, and he could easily envision the disapproving look his nanny would send his way.

She believed he was too lenient with Abby. But being too hard on her wasn't the answer either. He needed another option, because his heart and his head weren't on the same page at all.

The thought circled in the back of his mind as he guided his daughter into a pew midway down the aisle. He hadn't been in the sanctuary since his father's funeral. Now he wondered why it had taken him so long to come back. This church was his spiritual home. He'd attended Peace Community since he was a baby. He knew every room, every window, even every electrical wire. His dad and brothers had rewired the building five years ago.

He glanced over at Abby sitting beside him on the padded pew. Taking Abby to his church home should have been his first priority after bringing her back to Dover. So why had he been avoiding this place?

A few rows in front he saw Linc sitting with Gemma and Evan. They looked happy. Gil tried to squash the twinge of envy that surfaced. His brother deserved all the happiness he'd found.

The music began and he stood, opening the hymnal, smiling when he realized it was one of his favorites. Was it the Lord's way of saying welcome home? He held the book low so Abby could read the words as he sang out, wanting her to understand that lifting your voice in praise and worship was an important part of the service. He missed singing. He'd been a member of the men's chorus before his dad had died and played guitar in the praise band now and then. He'd stopped singing after the funeral. Everything had changed.

The sermon lifted a fog from his thoughts, shining a light on his darker emotions. He couldn't blame God any longer for the pain of the past. But that still left an ocean full of anger and resentment he'd carried for a long time. And he had no idea how to let any of that go.

Gil found himself looking around the congregation for Julie as they left the church. Had she come to the early service? Or had she changed her mind and stayed home?

Linc had invited them to have lunch at the Pine View Restaurant at Lake Shiloh. But first they had to run by the house and check on Ruffles. He had decided Linc got the better end of the puppy deal. Evan's dog, Champion, was already house trained, having lived with a family until they'd moved away. He had gotten stuck with a new puppy that had no sense at all. The only thing going for it was that Abby loved the black critter with her whole heart.

He debated whether to invite Julie to join them for lunch but decided against it. She might be working for him, but she deserved her time off. She'd already given up part of her Saturday to help with the puppy.

Lunch was nice. Abby seemed to be warming up to Evan now that they had their dogs to talk about. Watching his brother and Gemma together, the loving touches, the tender glances, unleashed a longing in him for the same. He realized that he and Leah had never really had the kind of happiness he saw between Linc and Gemma.

He'd fallen in love with Leah instantly, but their relationship had always been rocky. He'd wanted desperately to please her and make her happy, but it had proved an ever-moving target. There was always something else that would make her happy, a big house, a baby, a newer car. By the time he'd grasped the reality of her illness, it was too late. She was gone and so was Abby.

Julie tapped on the back door of the Montgomery house Monday morning, eager to start the day. The garage apartment had proved to be a cozy, peaceful place. She'd been afraid that being so close to Abby would distract her from resting. But once she'd settled in, she was able to focus on her online students and continue her preparations for the move without interruptions. The one thing she couldn't overcome was the secret she was keeping. Her conscience had pricked like barbed wire after attending church yesterday.

She'd heard the Montgomerys come and go a few times but managed to resist watching them. It was enough to know she was here, close by in case they needed her.

The door opened abruptly, and a very tired Gil stared back at her, his eyes wide, his expression one of befuddlement. "Is everything all right?"

He nodded. "Yeah. Come on in. We're running late."

The kitchen was a mess of dishes and cereal boxes. Ruffles scurried around her feet, begging to be petted. She scooped her up and cuddled her close. "Anything I can do?"

Gil pointed at the dog and glared. "That mutt is a menace. I should never have agreed to get a dog."

She was beginning to get the picture. "She's been keeping you up at night?"

Gil's anger deflated. "Whines all night. Makes

messes in the house and chewed up two sets of blueprints in my office."

"Is she still sleeping in Abby's room?"

He nodded. "Every time I even suggest putting the dog downstairs, Abby falls apart."

"You're the father. It's your job to set rules and boundaries. Losing sleep isn't good for either of you."

"I know, but I can't stand to see her so upset. She loves that dog."

"She'll get over it. You have to think of what's best for her and not let her have her way in everything."

Gil's blue eyes darkened, and he squared his shoulders. "She's been through enough. I'm not ripping that puppy from her arms. She just needs more time. I don't expect you to understand." Grabbing his jacket from the back of a kitchen chair, Gil picked up his briefcase and faced her. Before he could speak, Abby entered the room.

"'Bye, Daddy." She walked past him and pulled the puppy from Julie's arms, nuzzling it against her neck.

"'Bye, sweet pea. I'll see you tonight."

Julie watched his eyes as they rested on Abby. He wanted to hug her to tell her he loved her, but he didn't. When he met Julie's gaze, she saw the sadness and confusion in the blue depths and her heart longed to help. A muscle in his jaw flexed. Without another word he left.

It took great effort for Julie to get Abby into the car for school. She refused to accept that Ruffles couldn't ride to school with them and glared when Julie made her take Ruffles out into the yard to take care of business. It wasn't hard to see that the joy of having a puppy was wearing thin when it came to the more boring responsibilities of pet care.

It was only after Julie promised to play with Ruffles during the day that a grumpy Abigail climbed into the car. Clearly the lack of sleep was becoming more of an issue. She needed to have a talk with Gil, but his response to her suggestion this morning hadn't been well received.

Julie pulled into the drive after dropping Abby off at school, noticing that the car behind her pulled into the driveway next door. As she glanced in that direction, a woman got out and waved to her.

"You must be the Montgomerys' nanny. I've seen you dropping Abby off at school."

"Yes, I am." She met the woman at the edge of the front yard.

"Stephanie Fulton. My daughter Hannah is in Abby's class. She talks about Abby all the time. I was hoping Hannah and Abby could have a playdate. She's anxious to meet the new puppy."

"Really? That's nice to hear. I was afraid Abby didn't have many friends. She's recently come to live with her father, and the adjustment has been difficult."

"Abby is welcome to come over to our house anytime."

"Thank you. Having a friend nearby would be good for Abby. I'll speak with her father about it."

"Gil knows us from church, so it shouldn't be a problem."

After promising to get the girls together soon, Julie said goodbye and went inside. Making friends could help with Abby's shyness. She'd been a lot like Abby as a child: shy, quiet and with few friends. She was still that way. One of the hardest things she faced with her move was leaving DiDi behind and having to make new friends in France.

Having a classmate next door was ideal for Abby. She'd talk to Gil to make sure he was all right with the idea. She'd have to take care on how she approached the subject. His overprotective nature toward Abby could hinder her adjustment.

Gil was reluctant to take her advice on his child. She couldn't blame him. She was, after all, only the nanny.

Chapter Five

Gil glanced up as his brother Linc entered their father's office at the Montgomery Electrical Contractors building Monday morning. They had agreed that Gil would take over the main office, since he would be handling the business end of the company and Linc would continue to work out of his smaller office across the hall. As the more on-site part of the team, he didn't need the larger space. It was a practical solution, but Gil doubted if he'd ever feel comfortable sitting in his father's chair and trying to fill his shoes.

"I'm heading out to Meridian this afternoon to check on the Johnson house." He sat down, narrowing his gaze. "What's going on? You look like you haven't slept in days."

He held up two fingers. "Nights."

"Let me guess. Whiny puppy, right? Bro, you have to get control of that situation or you'll be useless."

"You sound like Julie. She thinks I should be harder on Abby."

"Harder? Or more firm? Like Dad was with us."

"Abby's not like us. She didn't have the same upbringing. Our relationship is sketchy enough. I'm not going to push her further away."

Linc leaned forward. "I understand. This fatherhood thing is new to me, too. I'm having to learn Gemma's rules for Evan's behavior. I can relate to him as a coach, but I'm still feeling my way with how to be a good dad to him. At least you were Abby's dad from the start."

"When she was a baby. But she's like a stranger now, and I feel like I'm swinging at air balls. Nothing I do connects."

"Maybe your nanny has some suggestions. She's had a lot of experience with kids."

Gil set his jaw. "Teaching them, not raising them. Big difference. I'm her father. I know what's best for her."

"But you just said you're having trouble connecting. Maybe an impartial observer can see things in a way you can't." Linc tilted his head and studied him. "Or is there something else going on?"

"Like what?"

He shrugged. "Like maybe you don't want to ask the nanny for advice because it'll make you look like you're incompetent or not in control?"

"Why should I care what the nanny thinks?"

"Because she's pretty and she knows how to connect with Abby, and I think she knows how to connect with you, too."

"You've been sipping those energy drinks again because you are talking crazy."

"I don't know. There's an unusual note in your voice when you talk about Julie. Very curious is all I'm saying."

Gil's cell phone rang, and he glanced at the screen.

Oak Grove Elementary. He looked at Linc before he picked up the phone. Abby's teacher explained the situation, sending a lead weight into the pit of his stomach. He ended the call, staring down at his clasped hands.

"What is it?"

"That was Abby's teacher. Abby pushed a boy down in the hallway. I have to go meet with the teacher. Can you postpone your trip until tomorrow?"

"Sure. Anything I can do?"

"I wish there was."

An hour later Gil pulled up at his house, tired, confused and at a loss on what to do. He reached for the bag of sandwiches he'd picked up. He hoped Julie was hungry.

She was curled up with her tablet on the living room sofa, Ruffles snuggled at her feet. She stood when she saw him, her expressive brown eyes widening with concern.

"What's wrong? Is Abby okay? What's happened?"

He shrugged out of his sport coat and gave her a reassuring nod. "Abby's fine, physically, but we do need to talk. I brought lunch." She searched his face, the worry bringing small creases to her forehead. He had the sudden urge to smooth them away. Her skin looked so soft, he knew it would feel like satin against his fingers. He averted his gaze and opened the bag. "Let's eat this while it's hot and I'll explain."

Settled at the table, he searched for a good place to begin. Swallowing his pride would be a sensible starting point. "I got a call from Mrs. Taylor earlier this morning."

"Abby's teacher? Why?"

"She pushed another student down." The shock on

Julie's face mirrored his own. "The boy was trying to take her backpack away and tore the strap. She got mad and shoved him."

"Poor baby. That backpack is precious to her."

Gil took a deep breath. "I wanted to bring her home, but the teacher felt it was best to let her finish out the day. There's more. Mrs. Taylor told me Abby is behind in several of her subjects. Math mainly. She suggested I find a tutor for her. She thinks Abby is bright, but lacking a solid foundation in basics."

"That's an easy fix. I can tutor her after school each day."

"I can't ask you to do that."

"I don't mind. I'd love to help out."

Her eagerness warmed his heart. She continually amazed him. She was always ready to help, always positive, supportive, and she did it with warmth and kindness. Maybe Linc had a point. He didn't like admitting his failings to Julie. He didn't understand why, but he wanted her to think well of him. But this wasn't about him, it was about Abby. He exhaled a slow breath. "I'm stumped. I don't know what to do for her. She's not getting better, she's getting worse. I want to fix things for her, to make her happy."

"Abby isn't a leaky faucet or a broken toy you can repair."

He pinched the bridge of his nose, knowing that what he was about to ask would be admitting he was a failure as a father. But Julie knew his child better than anyone. He looked into her pretty brown eyes and saw compassion. "I need your help. My way of doing things doesn't seem to work. Even my brother thinks

I'm doing everything wrong. She'll listen to you. You understand her better than I do."

"That's because I'm a professional."

"Where do I start?"

"Children need consistency and predictability. She needs rules and boundaries. You're her father, not her friend. Start with the biggest problem."

"Ruffles." She stifled a laugh, causing her dimple to appear.

"Perfect. Decide what needs to be done, explain it to Abby, then don't back down. Even if she cries or gets upset. She'll push back. Hard at first, but once she sees that you are serious she'll come around."

"I don't want to do anything to damage her self-esteem."

She shook her head. "Self-esteem doesn't come from lavishly praising a child for each little accomplishment or rescuing them from unpleasant situations. It comes from teaching them to solve problems, letting them fail then showing them they are loved whether they succeed or not. Then you give them a chance to try again."

Reaching across the table, she took his hand. "It's obvious how much you love her. She'll come to see that, too. But you have to be present in her life. Be there to listen, to hug, to guide and lift her up when she falls."

Gil squeezed her hand. It felt good in his. Her slender fingers were soft and strong. Like the woman they belonged to. "Be her hero."

"Exactly. But not her knight. Knights rush in and rescue the damsel, and she doesn't participate at all. Heroes come to her aid, lend their strength to the battle and protect you."

He wanted to be Julie's hero. To protect her, to lend

his strength if needed. "Is that what your father taught you?" The light in her eyes died, replaced with deep sadness. She never talked about her family, and now he wondered why.

"Yes. He taught me a lot. He was always there to support me."

She pulled her hand from his, and he resisted the impulse to take it again. "What else?"

Julie brushed her hair behind her ears. "Structure and routine are important. And tradition. Something you do together. Like breakfast every morning or a movie night. You could call her every day when she's home from school to let her know you are thinking about her. Commit to being home for supper each night, even if you have to go back to the office afterward. Give her something to depend on."

"My dad had a special time for all five of us. I don't know how he managed it, but he did."

"What about signing Ruffles up for an obedience class at the pet shop? You and Abby could learn to train the puppy together. She might not resent the changes so much if she knew you weren't mad at her dog."

Gil let his gaze travel over the appealing softness of her face. Once again she'd come up with the perfect solution to his problem. "That's a good idea." This time he reached out and took her hand. "I'm glad you took this assignment. You've been a blessing to us. I'll never be able to repay you."

Julie blanched and tugged her hand from his. Gil tried to figure out what he'd said that disturbed her. He'd meant to pay her a compliment.

"It's almost time to pick up Abby, and I have a few

errands to run before that. Unless you'd like to get her today."

He pushed up from the table. "Let's keep to the routine. I need to get back to the office. But I'd like you to be here when I talk to Abby about these school issues. We'll do that after supper."

"All right."

He watched Julie hurry out the door, a sense of unease settling in his chest. The last thing he wanted to do was upset her. He needed her. Abby needed her. Maybe that was the problem. He was starting to depend on her too much, and it made her uncomfortable. He'd been too forthcoming. From now on he'd take a step back and keep the employer/employee boundaries in place. He couldn't afford to lose Julie when she was making such progress with Abby.

Julie watched Abby's expressions closely that evening as the three of them sat around the table. Hoping to ease the situation, she'd taken it upon herself to prepare a nice dinner. She would have preferred to be in her little apartment during this serious discussion, but Gil had asked her to be present, claiming her connection with Abby would be helpful. More likely it was for his own moral support. Setting down rules for his daughter was a scary prospect for him. She understood completely. But he didn't understand that her emotional involvement was as deep as his own. Knowing her little girl was in for a serious behavior correction sent her stomach flip-flopping.

Abby listened to her father, her big brown eyes wide with confusion and a hint of tears as he laid out the new rules for Ruffles.

"You mean I can't play with her anymore?"

"You can play with her all you want. But from now on she sleeps in her crate down here in the laundry room. Not in your room. In the morning you can come and let her out, feed her and take her outside."

Abby's bottom lip jutted out. "But she'll be lonely."

"Not for long. That's why you and I are going to take Ruffles to the pet store and learn how to teach her to behave herself. Once she's trained, then she can spend more time in your room."

Abby glanced down at her pet. "She'll be sad."

"Maybe for a little while, but she'll learn that she has to mind you. How would you feel if she got loose and into the street? If she doesn't learn to obey and come when you call her, she could get hurt." Fat tears became deep sobs. Gil glanced at Julie and his distress matched hers. "It's for her own good. It's only for a little while. Think about the fun we'll have teaching her to sit and stay."

"And roll over?"

"Once she learns to obey, you can teach her all kinds of fun tricks."

The tears stopped, but the pout remained. Julie took her hand. "I'll be with Ruffles all day while you're at school. I won't let her get lonely."

Gil clasped his hands together, his expression serious and stern. "Now. Let's talk about what happened at school."

Abby drew her knees up in the chair, wiping tears from her eyes with the heel of her hand. "He tore my backpack."

"Why did he do that?"

She shrugged. "He called me stupid 'cause I always carry it. He said it was ugly."

Julie reached over and picked up the polka-dot bag. The strap had been ripped away from the fabric. She sent a pointed look at Gil.

"We can fix it, sweet pea. It'll be as good as new. I understand how upsetting it was for you, but you cannot push other people because you don't like what they say or do. It's wrong. Do you understand?"

Abby started to cry again.

Julie had another idea. She hesitated, then remembered Gil had wanted her here to offer advice. "Abby, since this backpack is so special, maybe it should stay here at home so all your treasures will be protected. You and I could go shopping for a new one that's just for school. Then you wouldn't have to worry about it."

Abby, who'd buried her head in her crossed arms, nodded.

"One more thing, Abby. Mrs. Taylor tells me you need help with math. Miss Julie has agreed to tutor you after school until you get caught up."

"I hate math."

Julie could barely make out the muffled statement. "I did, too. I had to work extra hard at it. Don't worry, you and I will figure it all out."

Abby lifted her head and looked at Gil, tears streaming down her face. "Are you going to send me away?"

Julie sucked in a breath, pressing a hand against her mouth. She ached to pull her child into her arms and reassure her. But there was no need. Gil was at her side in an instant, drawing her up into his arms.

"No, sweet pea. I would never send you away. I love you. I'm your daddy. I want you with me all the time."

Gil settled back into a chair, keeping Abby in his lap and brushing damp strands of hair from her face. Ruffles raised her paws and stared at them both. "Don't cry, honey. Everything is going to be fine. I promise."

The tender moment twisted deep into Julie's heart. She wanted to cradle her baby close and reassure her, but that was Gil's role. Quietly she stood and slipped out. The walk across the drive and up the stairs took all the strength she had. Safely inside her cozy home, she curled up on the sofa and released the emotions she'd been holding in check.

She should be shouting for joy. Gil had handled the situation firmly, with love and gentleness. Many of her concerns had been put to rest this evening. Gil would be a wonderful father, and his worries would fade quickly now. Abby had turned a corner, too. Watching Gil cradle his child had triggered a flood of conflicting emotions, pulling her heart in different directions. She'd been prepared to act as negotiator, helping them work through the issues and being a comfort to Abby.

She'd expected this tug-of-war with Abby. But what she hadn't anticipated was the way her attraction for Gil was growing. He was a good man. Warm, caring and determined to make his child happy. She couldn't have created a better parent for her child. He was everything she could have hoped for. A man she could fall in love with. A man she could *never* fall in love with. But if she wasn't vigilant, she'd end up falling for a man she couldn't have.

Needing perspective on the emotional night, Julie called DiDi.

"Finally you're talking sense. Yes, I think you should get out of there. The longer you stay, the greater the risk that the truth will come out. Why are you even asking me about this? You know what you should do."

"It's not that simple. She's facing all these new guidelines and having to be tutored after school, and not having her puppy in her room at night."

"And you don't think her dad can handle that?"

"Of course he can. He loves Abby. You should have seen him tonight. He would do anything for her. He was gentle and kind and reassuring. I know in time they'll be very close."

"Julie. Tell me you're not falling for this guy. You know that can't happen, don't you?"

She wanted to deny her feelings, but she couldn't. "I won't deny that I'm attracted to him. He's handsome and kind and he loves my daughter. But that's all it is. Appreciation."

"Uh-huh. Keep telling yourself that. I haven't heard this tone in your voice since you dated that guy you met at church a while back."

"That was years ago."

After reassuring her friend again that her heart was safe from the charming Gil Montgomery, she said goodbye, knowing deep down it wasn't completely true.

Needing a distraction from her guilty thoughts, she looked around for her tablet, realizing she'd left it at Gil's. She hated to intrude again, but Abby should be in bed now. Gil would understand if she slipped in to retrieve it. Besides, she'd like a moment to talk to him. She was curious how Abby had been after she'd left. It had nothing to do with a desire to be close to Gil again.

Gil sat on the edge of the bed watching his daughter cuddle with her puppy. She hugged her to her neck, stroked her wavy fur and pouted the whole time. Abby's big brown eyes were sad and worried as she looked up at him. He reached out and smoothed his palm over her hair. "She'll be fine, Abby. Trust me. I won't let anything bad happen to Ruffles."

Resigned, Abby handed the wiggly animal over. Gil held her close to his chest, scratching under the puppy's chin. "Just think how happy she'll be to see you in the morning."

He placed a kiss on Abby's forehead. "I love you, sweet pea." He knew better than to expect a response, but he prayed that someday she'd say she loved him, too.

After securing Ruffles in the crate, he went to the family room, hoping to distract his thoughts with a ball game. As he aimed the remote toward the TV, his gaze fell on the acoustic guitar resting in its stand in the corner. He hadn't touched the instrument in over a year. Music had always been his escape, his way of dealing with emotions. Playing had helped him sort through things and put him back on solid ground.

He hadn't felt like hearing any soothing chords in a long time. There had been too much pain and loss in his life lately. But tonight he'd experienced his first ray of hope. He'd dreaded drawing boundaries for Abby, fearful she would withdraw even more. But Julie's advice had been on target. Abby had endured the changes better than he'd expected. His heart still twisted when he remembered her fear that he would send her away. She'd allowed him to hold her and ease her worries. He'd never felt more like a father than in that moment. To be able to assure his child that she was safe and loved meant the world to him.

Julie had slipped away. He understood she'd wanted to give them privacy, but he'd wanted her to stay. She was a part of their lives now.

Picking up the guitar, Gil sat on the edge of the chair, resting the instrument on his legs and wrapping his hand around the neck. His fingers found a chord, and he lightly ran his thumb over the strings. As he began to play an old hymn, his turmoil drifted away. Softly he sang the words, about remembering to go to the Lord in prayer.

Maybe it was time to rejoin the men's chorus and volunteer for the praise band.

"Gil?"

He looked up to find Julie standing in the opening to the family room. "Hey. I didn't hear you come in."

"I knocked, but you didn't answer. I left my tablet here. I heard singing and got curious."

He rested his arm on the guitar. "I used to play all the time. I haven't had much reason to rejoice until recently." Movement from the hallway entrance into the family room caught his attention. "What's wrong, sweet pea? Are you okay?"

"I heard the music."

"Did I wake you? I'm sorry." Abby came toward him slowly, never taking her eyes from the instrument. "Would you like to see my guitar?" When she drew close, he tilted it a bit. "Take your finger like this and drag it across the strings."

She did, bringing forth a less than pleasant sound, but Gil's heart swelled inside his chest to the point he thought it would break his ribs. "That's it."

"Maybe Abby would like to hear a song."

He'd almost forgotten Julie was there. Almost. There

was always a faint scent of spring and sunshine in the air when she was near. She always seemed to know how to handle any situation. "Good idea." He searched for something simple that a child would know. "How about 'Jesus Loves Me'?"

He fingered a chord and started to sing softly. Abby stared at him with a puzzled expression. "You don't know this song?" When she shook her head, his joy washed away like a chalk painting in the rain, leaving behind evidence of another failure as a parent. He'd been so busy feeling sorry for himself he'd failed to consider what was best for Abby. He'd introduced her to church. Next he'd make sure she attended Sunday school.

Julie sat on the fireplace hearth nearby, holding out her hand to Abby. "Gil, I've forgotten the words to that song. Maybe you could help me and Abby to learn it?"

The warm rush through his veins quickened his heart rate. He captured Julie's gaze and smiled. "Sure."

A half hour later, Abby had learned the song and was tucked into bed again. Gil had asked Julie to remain. She glanced up at him from the sofa when he returned to the family room. "How did you know what to do?"

She shrugged. "I just put myself in her place. It feels awful to be left out, not knowing something everyone else does."

He sat at the other end of the couch. "Thank you."

"She's warming up to you, to being here."

"I guess she is. But that might be more your influence than mine."

"She was picking at the piano keys the other day."

"That must have sounded rotten. I haven't had it tuned in years. It was my grandmother's."

"Abby may have an interest in music. I'd keep an eye out for that. It could be another way to connect with her."

He looked into her eyes, inexplicably drawn to the warmth in her gaze. He didn't want her to go. She had come into his family as if she'd been designed specifically for them. Thoughts of entering into another relationship with a woman had been nonexistent. But Julie made the idea appealing.

"I told her we'd paint her room this weekend. She seemed excited." His voice sounded strange to his ears, higher-pitched than normal. His heart was beating erratically, too. Maybe it had something to do with the way the dim lights in the living room softened the line of her cheek and highlighted the sparkle in her eyes.

"If it's all right with you, I'll take her shopping for a new bedspread and curtains."

"That would be good. I'm sure I wouldn't have a clue."

She held up her tablet. "I have some students to teach."

Gil walked her to the door. She reached for the knob at the same time he did, and he found her in the circle of his arms. Her sweet scent seeped into his senses, muddling his thoughts. He looked into her warm brown eyes and his pulse jumped. His gaze traveled from her pretty eyes to the soft curve of her cheek and the slender column of her neck. Her pulse was beating rapidly. Like his.

"Julie, you've made a big difference in my life. I can never thank you enough for what you're doing for us."

She blinked, inhaling slowly. "Abby's happiness is important to me, too."

"I think you care about everyone's happiness. You have such a loving heart." Gently he touched her cheek, and it was softer than he'd imagined. Their eyes locked. The air in the room stilled. His gaze lingered on her beautiful expressive eyes, then traveled along her delicate cheeks to her kissable mouth. He knew he shouldn't kiss her, but the draw was too powerful to resist. He touched her lips, a feather-light kiss meant to tell her—what? I'm attracted to you? I appreciate you? He opened his eyes, his heart thudding at the soft look in her eyes. Then it was gone, replaced with wide-eyed surprise. She tugged on the door handle, forcing him to step back. "Gil. I'm glad I could help, but I'm just the nanny. And I'm moving to Europe soon."

"I'm sorry. You're right. I shouldn't have done that."

"It's okay. I didn't stop you, but it can't happen again. You understand that, don't you?"

"Yes, of course. I hope I haven't ruined things. Between us, I mean."

"No. Of course not. I'm here for Abby. We both want her to be happy. That's all we should be thinking about."

"Right." She stepped outside, triggering the motion light. Gil watched her walk across the drive and up the apartment steps before turning away. What had he been thinking? He hadn't made such a stupid move since he was in college.

But she'd kissed him back. He wasn't that out of practice that he didn't know that much. Before she backed off, he'd seen a flash of fear in her eyes. Surprise, he could understand. He'd caught her off guard.

But where did the fear come from? It didn't matter. He couldn't afford to take his attention from the main issue. Abby. There was no room for himself right now. Time for that later.

Chapter Six

Julie hurried into her apartment and locked the door. It was a pointless gesture, but it gave her a sense of protection and safety. Her heart raced, warming her skin. She touched her lips, reliving the brief touch of Gil's mouth on hers. What had she been thinking? She'd told herself to back away. But when she'd looked into his eyes, she'd been powerless to prevent it. Because she'd wanted it. Closing her eyes, she tried to think rationally. She shouldn't read anything into that brief kiss. Nothing at all. He was feeling grateful and overjoyed to see Abby taking an interest in something and learning the song. He probably saw her as the catalyst, and in his happiness he'd kissed her. Like a friend.

It would be easy to believe that if she weren't so attracted to Gil Montgomery. She'd felt drawn to him from the moment he'd opened the door that first day. She'd told herself it was because he was a very attractive man. But the more she got to know him, the more she admired him. But falling for the man was beyond dangerous.

This had to end. Scooping up her cell, she placed a

call to Agatha, only to be shuffled to voice mail. Exhaling a deep sigh, she hung up, then curled up on the couch. She'd try again later.

Five minutes later her cell phone rang, and she checked the screen, her shoulders sagging. Her mother. The last person she wanted to talk to. They hadn't spoken in nearly a year, and that was only because she'd wanted her parents to know she was moving overseas. As she'd expected, they hadn't seemed upset or even interested. Her mother had filled her in on her sister's condition and her father's health issues, then ended the call. As if shoveling a load of guilt on Julie's head would somehow bring her back into the fold.

Her comments to Gil about her father drifted through her mind. He'd been her hero growing up. He'd call her after school each day just to say hello, and on clear nights they'd look through his telescope at the stars and talk about things. She missed him. More so since coming to the Montgomerys and seeing Abby and Gil together. Being a part of their family dynamic was peeling away the protective covering around her heart she'd placed there years ago. Maybe, once she was finished here, she should go to Pensacola and see her family before she left for Paris. DiDi was right. It was time to deal with the past.

The cell stopped ringing. Should she call back? Not tonight. She had more pressing matters on her mind. Like how she was going to continue as Abby's nanny when she was so distracted by Gil, and how she was going to hide her attraction from him.

She touched her fingers to her lips again, unable to forget the kiss. She should have stopped it. But all she could think about at the time had been how close he was, how wonderful he smelled and how much she wanted to be in his arms. But instead of satisfying her curiosity, the kiss had only made her want to kiss him again.

Gil stared at the blueprints. He'd calculated the numbers for the project twice, but before he could write them down, they'd flown out of his mind. His lapse in judgment the other night still had him tied in knots. Kissing Julie was a big mistake, and his weakness might have cost him more than simple embarrassment. It might be the thing that chased Julie away. The last thing he wanted.

Abby loved her, depended on her and, more important, trusted her. As much as he wanted to be a father to his child, he was still feeling his way with their relationship. He needed Julie's wisdom and guidance. Now he'd put that at risk by giving in to a moment of temptation.

He looked up as his brother walked into the office. "I thought you were on your way to Winona to check on the Hunters' house."

"I am, but I want to talk first." He eased down into a chair. "Are you okay? You look like a man with a burden."

Having a brother so close in age had its drawbacks. He could read him like a book. "I'm fine."

Linc raised his eyebrows. "You're a terrible liar, bro. Things okay with Abby and you?"

"Getting better. The dog helped a lot. We started obedience classes last night, and she seems to enjoy it."

"That's good. Right?"

"Yes, but Abby is still resistant to me. She goes to

Julie for everything. She pinched her finger the other day, and she would only allow Julie to take care of it, even though I was right beside her when it happened."

"Maybe it's time to get a new nanny."

"No. Julie and Abby have a special relationship. I think that's important right now. She doesn't need any more changes. Besides, Julie is very wise and compassionate. She has a real gift with children." He glanced over at Linc. There was a knowing smile on his face that Gil didn't like at all. "What?"

"That was a pretty glowing endorsement for your nanny. Is there something else you want to tell me?"

Gil dropped his gaze to the desktop, shuffling papers around. What would Linc say if he told him what had happened between him and Julie? It was just a brief kiss, but it had touched something deep in him that he didn't understand. He wasn't a romantic man. He liked things simple, rules and directions laid out clearly in black and white. He'd met his wife, fallen in love and never looked back. Something about Julie shifted his perspective. He found himself thinking about her smile, the way her dark hair swayed when she moved and how her expressive milk chocolate eyes beckoned him. That was something he would never reveal. "What did you want to see me about? I've got to get this job figured by tonight."

Linc chuckled. "I know when you're avoiding, but I'll let it slide for now. I wanted to know if you'd heard from Al on that Baton Rouge project. I'd expected to hear from him by now."

Al Thompson was an important general contractor and a longtime friend of their father's. When a developer was lining up a project, Al could always be counted on to recommend them as the electrical contractors. Not because of the friendship, but of the dependability of Montgomery Electrical. They were counting on his continued support to get through the slump the company was in. "No. Not a word."

"Me either. That's not like him. Maybe I should give him a call and see what's up. We need a couple of these big jobs to come our way. We can't make it with only the residential side of the company."

"Let me know what you find out."

Linc stopped at the door. "Oh, and I'm going over to the farmhouse to salvage what I can. You want to help?"

"Sure. Just let me know when."

Gil redirected his focus to the numbers in front of him. He should be searching for potential jobs to bid on. Linc was right; if things didn't start going their way soon, he wasn't sure if the business their grandfather started would survive.

Placing his elbows on the desk, he rested his head in his hands, unable to stop thinking about the kiss he'd shared with Julie. Maybe he was losing his mind. Or suffering from the stress of worrying about Abby.

Or maybe he was a man who was attracted to a lovely woman. He had no idea what to do about it. One thing he knew for sure. He would avoid any time alone with Julie and pray she didn't decide to leave. And he'd keep his mind on helping his daughter and nothing else.

Julie had descended the last step from her apartment when she heard someone call her name. Nancy Scott hurried toward her. She stopped, resting her hand at her throat as she caught her breath.

"I'm so glad I caught you. I'm in desperate need of help. My cochair for the father-daughter event I told you about has fallen and broken her hip. Poor thing is going to be laid up for weeks. I need someone to organize the talent show, and I immediately thought of you."

She held a hand up in protest. "Oh, but that was for children at my school. Besides, I have a commitment to Mr. Montgomery to give all my time and attention to Abby."

"Don't you worry about that. This isn't a full-time job. I just need someone to get all the names together and figure out the order of the performers. There will be a few meetings in the evenings and weekends, and of course the night of the event." She sighed and took a deep breath. "I know this is sudden and you're new here, but there's no one else I can ask. Normally Francie, Gil's mother, would step in, but she's not here."

Julie weighed the pros and cons. She hadn't mentioned the talent part of the father-daughter event to Gil yet. But after seeing him play the guitar, she had decided to nudge him into entering himself and Abby. It would be a perfect way to draw them closer. Maybe if she were more actively involved, she could persuade them. "All right. I'd be happy to help. As long as I can do it during my off time from Abby. But I'll need to check with Gil first."

"Thank you, darling. You're an answer to my prayer. Having someone with experience will make the whole process so much easier."

By the time Julie left to pick up Abby from school, she'd formulated a plan on how to approach Gil about the talent show. He'd agreed to take his daughter to the dinner, but she had a feeling he wouldn't be too keen on entering the talent contest. It would be a wonderful opportunity for Abby and Gil to participate together. The problem was, things between her and Gil had been strained ever since the kiss.

It had been several days since their encounter, and he was definitely avoiding her. Not physically. That would have been impossible. But his attitude toward her had cooled considerably. He avoided eye contact as much as possible, directed most of his conversation to Abby and didn't initiate any with her at all. The longer the tension went on, the unhappier she became. She told herself it had nothing to do with her feelings for Gil. It was all about maintaining communication between them so they could make good decisions for Abby.

As soon as Abby had finished her math lessons, she went to play with Ruffles and Julie went to the kitchen to start supper. The past week had brought about another change, too. Evening meals with Gil and Abby. It had started as a special request from Abby and had quickly become the routine. Gil had encouraged her by pointing out that there was no need to fix separate meals when she was right across the driveway. She'd always loved to cook, but cooking for one was difficult. Fixing meals for Gil and Abby had renewed her interest. Now it was one of the highlights of her day.

Unfortunately tonight was her first meeting with the father-daughter event committee. She'd have to find another time to speak with him. Thankfully the meeting went quickly and, to her surprise, was thoroughly enjoyable. She looked forward to organizing the various acts, and she came away more determined to convince Gil to participate.

Peeking out the apartment window, she saw the

lights were still on in the family room. This might be the perfect time to talk to him. Abby should be in bed, and she could assure him she wasn't upset about the kiss. Even though that would be a lie. Her pulse still raced whenever she thought about it.

Flier in hand, she walked across the back deck and tapped on the French door. Gil was in the recliner, staring at the TV, but she had the impression he wasn't watching the program. He motioned her inside.

"Is everything all right?"

She liked the way he was always quick to be concerned. He had a compassionate heart. "I just came to talk to you for a moment."

Gil looked at the paper in her hand, his eyes widened. "You're not resigning, are you? If it's because of the…what happened…the other night. That was a mistake. I wasn't thinking. I didn't mean to step over the line."

"No." She held up her hand. "It's okay. I mean it wasn't… I wasn't…" She puffed out a breath. "This is about something else." She handed him the flier. "I think it would be a nice idea if you and Abby entered the talent contest."

Gil studied the paper. "And do what?"

She sat down. "You play the guitar and she can sing. She has a nice voice. So do you. It would be sweet."

He handed her back the flier. "No. I haven't played in front of people in a long time. I doubt Abby would want to. You know how shy she is."

"She's coming around, Gil. She talks about you, and she's even asked me a few questions. Like where you work and about your family. She looks forward to the obedience classes."

"Because of the pup."

"No, because of you. She reminds me all afternoon that she and her daddy are going to Ruffles's school."

"Really?" He smiled. "She asked me yesterday if I could teach her to play guitar. I suppose I could get her a small one, show her a few chords."

"That's perfect." She reached out and touched his forearm. "Gil, think of the trust it would create. Ruffles's classes are over soon, and this can be your new project together." She could see Gil warming to the idea.

"Do you think she'll go for it?"

"I'll give her a little nudge. Don't worry. Now that I'm organizing the talent show, I'm sure I can get Abby interested. And I'll be sure and give you a good slot in the lineup." She smiled and started to rise. Gil reached out and took her hand.

"I don't know if I could have gotten through this adjustment period without your help."

"Sure you could have."

"Do you get this involved with all your kids as a teacher and a nanny?"

Julie kept her eyes lowered as she shrugged. "It's hard not to when you're with them all the time." Or they happen to be your biological child.

"Why haven't you married, Julie? You're a natural mother. You should have kids of your own. You have so much love to give a husband and family."

She was blindsided by his comment, and her mood plummeted. She'd been told that before, but this time it was different. She'd love to have those things, but she'd lost that privilege eight years ago. She forced a smile and pulled her hand away. "Too busy with other people's children to have my own."

"That's a shame. You were made to be a mother."

Julie stood and gestured to the flier. "Let me know what you decide. I think it would be a wonderful thing for you and Abby to do together."

He held her gaze as if he wanted to say something else, something personal. The look in his blue eyes was the same one she'd seen the other night. The air between them vibrated. She couldn't ignore it any longer. The attraction between them was growing by the day. The sensible thing to do would be to leave. But like a fly trapped in honey, she wanted to enjoy as much of her time with him as possible. The memories would have to last her forever.

Julie settled at the front table at the Square Cup coffee shop so she could look out the window at the charming town of Dover. Since bringing Abby here for hot chocolate, she'd found the atmosphere perfect for reading her devotional book and organizing her thoughts for the day. She made it her first stop after dropping Abby off at school. Too much time at Gil's house churned up the guilt in the back of her mind and pointed up how comfortable she felt there. She was constantly torn between wanting to stay and make sure Gil and Abby were fully reunited, and the knowledge that she was keeping a big secret from them both. Particularly Gil. She knew his feelings about hiding the truth. She'd seen the pain in his eyes, heard the anger in his voice when he'd explained about his wife's deception.

Leah had been emotionally disturbed. Julie had

no such excuse. Only a misguided desire to ease her fears about her daughter. Movement pulled her from her thoughts, and she looked up as Sarah, the owner of the shop, stopped at the table with a plate of fresh cookies.

"You're becoming a regular."

"I guess I am. It's warm and friendly here." Except she couldn't ever become a regular patron. The clock was still ticking toward her move to Paris. She fingered the silver heart around her neck. It would be her only link to Abby when this assignment was done.

"That's my plan. I want my customers to feel—" Sarah inhaled sharply.

Julie watched as the color drained from the woman's face. Her gaze was riveted on the necklace Julie wore.

"Where did you get that?"

Julie's heart skipped a beat. She never knew how to answer that question when people asked. "It was given to me. A long time ago." Sarah's blue eyes clouded, and she sank into the chair, her hand at her throat. Julie watched as Sarah pulled out an identical filigree heart with a ruby birthstone in the center. She looked into Sarah's eyes and saw her own story written there.

Sarah glanced around. "The Phyllis May Foundation."

Julie's stomach heaved. This couldn't be happening. Of all the people to run into in a small town like Dover, she'd met someone who could expose the truth. Sarah must have seen her panic.

She laid her hand over hers. "It's okay. I won't say anything, and I didn't mean to scare you."

She clutched the necklace, her heart racing. "I've never met anyone with this necklace."

"Me either. How long ago were you at the foundation?"

"Almost nine years. I had a little girl."

"Seven for me. A boy." Sarah fingered the small heart. "I've thought about taking this necklace off and putting it away, but I'm afraid I'll forget my son."

"Me, too. I feel like I have her close to me when I wear it."

Sarah took her hand. "We don't ever have to talk of this again, but if you need someone, please call me."

Julie left the café as soon as Sarah walked off. Her hands shook as she made her way to the car. The risks were piling up. Now Sarah knew about her past. What if she told someone or accidently mentioned they had given up their babies? She doubted Sarah would share their secret, but it was one more thing to worry about. Her life was becoming more complicated, and she had no idea how to stop the forward motion.

Nancy wasted no time in getting Julie immersed in the preparations for the father-daughter dinner. She'd attended her first meeting the other night and been handed nearly a dozen applications for the talent show. Nancy had informed everyone that the response to the dinner was so large they might have to find a new venue since the church fellowship hall was already maxed out.

The more Julie became involved with the town, the more she felt at home here. In the past few days the weather had warmed again, and she'd taken the time to explore. Everywhere she went, people were eager to know how Gil and Abby were doing. The Montgomery family was loved and respected, and Julie knew the curiosity was born from a genuine concern for their fellow citizens.

If things had worked out differently, she could see herself putting down roots in this small town and becoming a part of the community. But her future was elsewhere. She would have to take comfort in the knowledge that her daughter would grow up in Dover.

Things between Gil and Abby were improving rapidly. Ruffles was becoming a well-behaved little fur ball, Abby was practicing her chords on the guitar and her grasp of math was nearly up to speed. The past few days she'd even greeted her father with a hug when he came home.

In a few weeks her assignment would be over. The thought dropped a dark cloud over her mood. Soon she would ride off into the sunset, leaving them both behind. She had a trunk full of precious memories to take with her now. She couldn't ask for more.

Julie parked her car near the garage late Saturday morning. Nancy had called a meeting first thing today to discuss the new location for the dinner. Being new in town, Julie had few suggestions to offer for alternate venues. She had several online students' papers to go over this afternoon, but first she wanted to check in with Gil and Abby.

Gil had promised they would paint Abby's room purple today, and she had talked of nothing else all week. Julie stepped into the kitchen and set her purse on the counter.

"No!"

Gil. Julie hurried toward the stairs. Had he fallen? Was he hurt? Before she could take the first step, Ruffles shot past her into the kitchen. A very purple Ruffles. Julie darted after her, scooping her up before she could drip paint on the family room carpet. Holding the animal at arm's length, she carried her to the laundry room and set her in the sink. "What have you done?"

The pup yelped, her dark eyes oozing guilt. Julie turned on the water and washed as much of the "Perfectly Perfect Purple" paint from the dog's fur as she could, dried her and secured her in the crate before grabbing up a roll of paper towels and heading back upstairs. She hated to think what Abby's room looked like. Or what the future might hold for one fuzzy little dog.

Julie wiped up as much of the paint puddles from the floor as she could as she went along, but the mess was bigger than paper towels could handle. Cautiously she peeked into Abby's room. Gil was sopping up spilled paint with a towel, and Abby was seated cross-legged on the bed, pouting. She had paint splatters on her face.

Gil glanced up, then sat back on his heels. "We had a little setback. Someone forgot to put Ruffles in her cage before we started."

"I'm sorry, Daddy."

He dragged the back of his hand over his forehead, leaving a fresh streak of paint. Julie stifled a giggle.

"It's okay. But I hope you see now why you can't let a puppy run around when we're trying to paint."

"I know."

Gil shrugged his shoulders. "It's only paint. I was planning on pulling out the carpet anyway. This will just hurry things along."

"I cleaned up Ruffles and put her in the crate. There's a trail of purple puppy paw prints down the hall and on the stairs."

He stood and picked up the paint tray, now piled with soaking purple towels. "I'm going to change clothes and get the shop vac out. Abby, you go downstairs with Julie and see if you can help her clean up some of this mess."

She nodded and scooted off the bed, glancing over her shoulder at the two freshly painted walls. "Thank you for my purple walls. I love them."

"You're welcome. We'll finish the other walls later."

Two hours later, Julie pulled up a chair at the table and studied Gil and his daughter. Gil looked exhausted after working to clean up all the paint. The floors were mainly tile and hardwood downstairs, but the upper hall and stairs were carpeted like Abby's room. Even the powerful shop vacuum couldn't remove all the paint. Abby kept glancing at her dad as if trying to judge how upset he was. Ruffles lay at her side, none the worse for wear, but looking guilty as anything. "I hadn't expected such excitement this morning. I can't wait to tell my friend DiDi about this."

Gil scowled, until he realized she was teasing. He smiled, flashing a row of white teeth and putting a twinkle in his deep blue eyes. Her breath lodged in her throat, and her insides melted into a soggy puddle. The man's smile should come with a warning label. Overexposure could be harmful to one's heart.

"Well, at least we got the color right."

Abby giggled and nodded. "It's beautiful."

He hugged her to his side. "Good. That's all that matters. My brother and I tried to paint our room once. Linc was too lazy to move the furniture, so he just painted around it. Our dad wasn't too happy. Especially since it was black paint."

"That sounds gross."

"It was." Gil squeezed Abby's hand. "I think we'll move you to the spare room for a few days until I can get the rest of the room painted and have that carpet pulled up."

"Okay. Can Ruffles stay with me?"

"I suppose." He looked at Julie. "I meant to ask you how the meeting went this morning."

"Fine, but we're trying to find a new place to hold the dinner. The number of people signed up for the meal has tripled, and there are nearly twice as many entrants to the talent show as last year. Nancy is thrilled, but the church can't hold that large a crowd. They're looking into using the VFW hall. They have a large enough kitchen, plenty of space for tables and the stage is large enough, but they don't think the electrical system can handle the extra power needed for the show."

"Well, that's not a problem. I can take care of that."

"You can?"

"Sure. I own an electrical contracting company. I'll swing by there tomorrow and take a look."

"That would be wonderful. Time is running out, and we need to get the venue established ASAP."

"Oh, and I keep forgetting to tell you that Abby has been asked to be the flower girl at my brother's wedding. She'll need to have the dress fitted. I was hoping you could handle that."

"I'd be happy to." She smiled at Abby. "A flower girl is a very special honor. Are you excited?"

"I don't know what it is."

"Oh, you'll love it. You get to wear a fancy dress

and toss rose petals in the church aisle as you lead the bride in."

"By myself?" She looked at Gil.

"No. Evan is the ring bearer, so you'll walk down together."

"Okay."

"Gemma said to call her if you have any questions. She'll give you the name of the dress shop and you can set up an appointment."

"I'll take care of it."

Gil stood. "I'd better make a few calls and have those floors replaced."

"I'm going to look at my new purple walls." Abby scooted off the chair.

"Don't go in the room. Just look."

"Okay."

Julie watched the pair move off, her heart trailing behind father and daughter. With each event she became more and more embedded in their lives. Tomorrow they would be laughing at the mess Ruffles made. She would take Abby for her fitting, work with her on math skills and make sure she had everything she needed each morning when she left for school. Mundane, everyday tasks performed by mothers everywhere day after day.

She'd done them herself in various assignments as a nanny. But this was different. This was her little girl. It was the life she'd allowed herself to contemplate only when she was at her lowest points. Now she was living it out in real time. Except it wasn't her life, or her home or her man. It was a fairy tale. She was dancing at the ball, but time would run out and she'd have to flee from the palace. She didn't even have a glass slipper to leave behind.

But she would leave the shattered pieces of her heart scattered on the ground.

Chapter Seven

Gil climbed from his mud-splattered vehicle and rolled his shoulders to work out the kinks. He and Linc had taken the day off to dismantle as much of the old family home as possible. Their great-grandparents had built the home when they first settled in Dover. His father had lived there until he'd married and built the large home Gil and his siblings had grown up in. Linc had sold the property to save the company on the condition that he could salvage anything reusable from the house.

Shoving his work gloves into his pocket, he opened the back door. His heart swelled with anticipation thinking about Julie being on the other side. With the puppy issues settled, life had fallen into a comfortable routine. He'd been surprised at how quickly Abby had stopped complaining about Ruffles not sleeping with her. Laying out boundaries for his daughter had changed everything. The first few days had been rough. The icy glares, the tears, the stomping off had threatened his resolve. But when Abby had realized none of her tantrums would change his mind, she'd resigned herself.

And it was all because of Julie. She glanced over her shoulder when he stepped into the kitchen. Her ever-present smile lightened his mood and eased the tightness in his muscles.

"You look like you worked hard today."

"We removed eight doors, five mantels and nearly a dozen windows." He arched his back. "And I'm paying for every one of them."

"What will happen to the rest of the house?"

Gil leaned a hip against the counter before plucking a grape from the fruit bowl. "A friend of ours will salvage the lumber that's reusable and store it at our mom's place."

"What does your brother plan on doing with all that wood?"

"Hopefully use it in the home he'll build for his family one day."

"That's nice. I think it would be wonderful to have pieces of your great-grandparents' home in your house."

The light that came into her brown eyes captured his full attention. Was Julie longing for roots? A family? He'd assumed she was happy being single, but now he wondered if she was settling for what she had instead of what she wanted.

"I'd better get cleaned up. Something smells good, and I'm starving."

"It'll be on the table when you get back down."

Her smile and easy manner filled him with a sense of belonging he'd missed. He fought the urge to kiss her cheek before he went upstairs. Instead he simply walked from the room, his insides going all warm and fuzzy. Obviously he'd overexerted himself today. He wasn't used to the physical labor. He'd feel better after he cleaned up.

The table was set and Abby was carefully filling the glasses with sweet tea when he returned to the kitchen. Julie had prepared spaghetti. One of his favorites. Abby said the blessing and they settled down to the meal. Gil allowed the warmth of the moment to enfold him, indulging in the feeling of family. It wasn't real, but it felt good nonetheless.

"Miss Julie, may I be excused? Ruffles has to go out."

"Yes, you may."

Gil caught the look of pride in Julie's eyes. Abby's manners were improving every day.

"It must have been hard for you and your brother to take the old house apart."

He nodded. Gil regretted selling his own piece of land to build Leah a huge house they didn't need and he no longer owned. But he didn't regret using some of the money to adopt Abby. "Linc hated to sell, but it saved the family business. I just hope it wasn't a stop-gap measure."

"What do you mean?"

"We're losing jobs we normally win. Al Thompson, the general contractor we deal with, was a close friend of our dad's. We could always count on him to steer jobs our way. Now, because of the near failure of the business last year, he feels we're a risk. But we never went bankrupt, and we finished that job on time. Thanks to Linc."

"Then convince him otherwise."

"I don't think words will sway this guy."

"Then you should go talk to him, face-to-face. Assure him you can do what your father always did."

"He lives in Houston."

Julie raised her eyebrows. "And what would he think of a business associate who went all that way to reassure him that his company was solid and capable of handling jobs the way they always had? Maybe, if you told him the circumstances, reminded him that you are your father's son, it would overcome his concerns."

Gil smiled, his gaze taking in her sincere expression. Once again she'd come up with the perfect solution. She always knew what he needed. Always had a simple answer to a problem, whether it was getting a little girl a puppy or standing up to a contractor. "You may have something there."

"I think you and your brother should both go. Present a united front. Your father may be gone, but he left two sons in his place who are capable and determined to carry on in his name. What have you got to lose?"

"Not a thing. All right. I'll talk to Linc about it first thing tomorrow."

"Ruffles! No! Come back."

Abby's shrill cries brought Gil to his feet. Abby burst through the patio doors, her eyes wide with fear, tears streaming down her cheeks. "Ruffles ran away. She chased Miss Nancy's cat and ran out the gate and she won't come back."

Abby ran to Julie's side. "You have to find her, Daddy."

Gil grabbed his jacket. "I'll find her."

Julie watched Gil race out the door, her heart a lead weight inside her chest. Abby's sobs deepened, and

Julie held her close, stroking her hair. "Don't worry. He'll find her."

"I want to help look for Ruffles."

"We'd better stay here in case she comes home. But we can check to see if she's hiding near the garage. Grab your jacket and let's go outside."

They checked around the garbage cans, behind the garage and in the front flower beds, but no Ruffles. It was dark, and trying to find a black dog in the gloom was hard enough, but the more they looked, the more upset Abby became.

She could hear Gil in the distance calling the dog's name. She tried not to think about what that might imply. The farther Ruffles wandered, the greater the danger. Cars, other people, bigger animals, all posed a threat. She shivered at the thought and tried to hide her worry from Abby.

"I'm sorry I didn't shut the gate. I called and called, but Ruffles didn't come back."

Julie hugged her close. "It was an accident. Dogs like to chase cats, and Ruffles got excited and forgot to obey you. Do you hear your daddy calling her? He'll find her and bring her back safe and sound. You'll see."

"Let's look around the garage again. Maybe she snuck back while we were out front." The sickening sound of screeching tires split the night air. Julie's heart froze. Abby appeared unaware of the sound. Hopefully she hadn't heard it or if she had, she didn't realize the implications. How would she explain to Abby what had happened? Her heart would be broken and there would be nothing Julie could do to make it better. She sent up a prayer that the horrible sound didn't mean a sad ending for Ruffles.

The air was too cold to let Abby stay out much longer. "Let's go inside and warm up, sweetheart. I'll make us some hot chocolate while we wait. Your daddy will need something warm to drink when he brings Ruffles home."

She stirred Abby's chocolate and set the cup on the table as the back door opened and Gil stepped inside. He held an unmoving black dog in his arms. She held her breath. Ruffles raised her head and barked, eliciting a squeal from Abby.

A tearful Abby pulled the puppy from her father's arms and held her close, rocking back and forth as she buried her face in the wavy fur. "I'm sorry, Ruffles." She drifted off to the living room.

Gil ran a hand through his hair. "When I heard those tires screech I thought for sure Ruffles was a goner."

She hurried to his side, slipping her hand in his. "Me, too. I didn't know how I was going to tell Abby."

Gil drew their clasped hands up to his chest. "Thankfully we don't have to."

Abby walked back into the kitchen, Ruffles at her heels. She looked at her father, her big brown eyes wide and a bit sad. "Thank you, Daddy, for finding Ruffles."

He tilted her chin upward. "You're welcome. But I hope this will be a lesson to you. You have to be more careful about the gate, and you'll need to work with your dog more on her obedience."

Abby teared up and reached for him. "Thank you."

Gil picked her up and held her close to his chest. "Of course, sweet pea. That's what daddies do."

Abby wrapped her arms around his neck and hugged him tight. "I love you, Daddy."

Julie's heart squeezed at the look of profound love

on Gil's face. She knew he'd waited a long time to hear those words from his daughter. She wiped tears from her cheeks. The final corner had been turned for Gil and Abby. She knew with certainty that they would be fine from here on.

Which meant she was no longer needed.

Gil hung up the phone, then leaned back in his office chair and breathed a sigh of relief. All the bids had been submitted, and he'd placed his last follow-up call. Now it was a waiting game. He offered up a prayer that at least one of the bids would result in a job. That would make him a happy man.

His gaze drifted to the picture of Abby and Ruffles he'd placed on his desk last week. What made him happier was the memory of Abby's declaration last night that she loved him. He couldn't stop smiling. He'd feared he'd never hear those sweet words from his daughter. And all because he'd rescued that black fur ball from being flattened by a car. Thankfully the driver had seen Ruffles dart off the sidewalk and stopped in time. He'd been very apologetic and upset that he might have hit the little mutt.

Linc peeked into the office, shaking his head and smiling. "You still feeling like a hero? That smile you're wearing has enough wattage to power the building."

Gil leaned forward. "Not a hero, but I do feel like a dad. Everything changed last night. I didn't think I'd ever reach this point with Abby."

"Saving a little girl's puppy is a big deal. I knew you'd figure out the father thing in time."

"I think Julie had more to do with it than I did. She

always knows what to do and how I should handle Abby."

Linc perched on the edge of the desk. "Don't sell yourself short. You've been working hard at establishing a relationship with Abby."

"Julie wants me and Abby to enter the talent portion of the Father-Daughter Night at the church. I think I'm going to if Abby agrees."

"After saving Ruffles I'm sure she'd agree to anything."

"I'm going by the music store this afternoon and picking up a small guitar just to sweeten the deal."

"I may have to volunteer to help out just so I can see you two onstage."

"There's one more thing I wanted to run by you." Gil quickly outlined Julie's suggestion about a face-to-face meeting with Al Thompson.

"That's a great idea. Dad and Al were always close. If we reminded him of that relationship, explain that a change in management is often rocky, he might come around. When do you want to go?"

"As soon as possible. You've worked with him more than I have. Will you set it up?"

Linc pointed at him and winked, then walked out.

Gil breathed out a slow sigh. Maybe his life was finally falling into place. He'd made progress with Abby, and there was new hope for the future of the company. That left only one big hole in his life. Someone to share all this happiness with. Someone like Julie. For a moment he allowed himself to imagine a future that included a family. One where love ruled, honesty existed and problems were discussed and resolved together.

He wondered if Julie weren't leaving for Paris, if

there might be a future together. He shrugged off the thought. He was moving too fast and in the wrong direction. He had Abby, and their relationship was all that mattered.

He pushed back from the desk, closed the computer and headed out. He had a small guitar to purchase before he went home. He wondered if they made them in purple.

The sound of Gil's vehicle pulling into the driveway sent Julie's heart tripping. Knowing he was home, that they would be sharing the evening meal, filled her with sweet contentment. In her heart she knew she was playing a dangerous game of pretend. Her dream of living in Paris, of exploring the most romantic city on earth, was beginning to lose its appeal. What she wanted to do was stay here with Gil and Abby and be part of their world. That would be the greatest thing she could imagine. But it was also her greatest nightmare, because if the truth ever came out, she'd lose them both and she would never recover.

She noticed the guitar the moment Gil stepped through the door into the breakfast room. She grinned. "Where did you find that? It's precious."

Gil held up the small instrument. "You think so? I'm hoping it'll encourage Abby to say yes to being in the talent show."

"Oh, good. You're going to enter. I'm so glad."

"Unless she says no."

"I don't think she will. She told me today that one of the girls in her class was excited because she and her daddy are entering. I think she'll be thrilled."

Ruffles skidded to a halt and placed her paws on

Gil's shin, begging for attention. Abby followed close behind, stopping and staring at the small guitar. She looked at her father for an explanation.

"I thought maybe you'd like to have a guitar of your own. One more your size that would fit your hands better."

Abby's smile widened, and she reached for the gift. "It looks like yours."

"Yes. It does. I couldn't find a purple one, but I did get you a purple strap." He handed the small bag to Abby. She pulled out the multihued purple strap and giggled.

"I love it. Thank you, Daddy." She went to him and hugged his waist. "Will you teach me to play?"

"I will, but first I have a question. What if you and I entered the father-daughter talent show at church? We could play our matching guitars and sing."

She nodded. "Carrie Sue and her dad are going to play the piano. Now I can tell her I'll be in it, too."

Gil rested his hand on her head. "But we'll have to practice hard. It's not that far away."

Julie's heart was overflowing. Seeing Gil and her daughter growing closer, sharing things, making memories, exceeded her expectations.

"Why don't you get started on the lessons and I'll get supper on the table."

The sounds of Gil's deep voice as he instructed Abby drifted into the kitchen and lingered in her heart. This was a perfect moment. Taking care of the people she loved. She closed her eyes, sensing her emotional roots burrowing deeper into the Montgomerys' world.

The moment dinner was over, Abby darted back to the family room and picked up her guitar. Gil hurried to join her, the joy on his face a beautiful sight to see. Julie longed to stay and watch the lessons, but tonight was another committee meeting and she needed to be there. Stepping into the family room, she heard Abby ask Gil who taught him to play the guitar. The sadness that passed over his features gripped her heart.

"My daddy taught me the way I'm teaching you."

"Where's your daddy?"

"He's in heaven."

Something in Gil shifted, a darkening that troubled her. She wondered if he'd ever grieved for his father. From what she could piece together, Gil had been hit with the loss of his dad, then the problems with his ex-wife a few weeks later. She wished there was something she could do for him.

Julie said goodbye, reminding them of her meeting, then went to her car. She might have trouble concentrating this evening. She couldn't shake the deep look of sadness she'd seen in Gil's blue eyes.

Thankfully the meeting went quickly. Everyone agreed to use the VFW hall since the entries to the talent show had grown. Gil had checked out the facility and had reported that putting in a subpanel should provide the extra power needed.

She debated whether to check on Gil before she went up to her apartment. She'd been unable to forget the look of profound sadness on his face when he'd spoken of his father. Perhaps she should maintain some distance. If he needed to talk, she felt sure he would seek her out.

After preparing for bed, she slipped on her favorite baggy sweater and stepped out onto the small balcony off the bedroom. The weather had warmed the past few days, and a hint of spring was in the air. In a few weeks the azaleas would start blooming. The yellow jasmine bush at the side of the garage was already budding.

She looked forward to seeing what spring would bring to the Montgomery yard. The bushes were all old and established and would offer a riot of color. Movement from below drew her gaze. Peering through the darkness, she could make out a figure sitting in one of the patio chairs. Gil. He leaned forward, elbows on his knees, his head cradled in his hands.

Alarm lanced through her and she started to call out. The broad shoulders started to shake. A deep groan rose on the night air. She sucked in a deep breath. Finally he was grieving for all he'd lost. She longed to go to him, comfort him, but this was a private moment.

Slowly she turned and went back inside, careful not to make any noise. Gil's grief triggered long-buried emotions of her own. He'd lost his father. She'd lost both of her parents, not to death, but to rebellious pride. Being Abby's caregiver had opened her eyes to things she'd not understood before. She'd been able to maintain a safe emotional distance with her students. Even though she became overly involved in their lives at times, they weren't her flesh and blood.

Her gaze landed on her smartphone sitting on the end table. Maybe it was time to reach out. Her mom had called twice during the time Julie had been at the Montgomerys', but she'd ignored the voice mails. Seeing Abby and Gil draw closer filled her with an ache to reconnect with her family. It was a situation she'd ignored far too long.

With a shaking hand, she pulled up the call list and touched the number labeled Mom. She fought the urge to hang up three times before a soft familiar voice answered. Tears burned her eyes. "Mom, it's me. J.J."

Her mother's voice cracked as she spoke. "Oh, my sweet girl. It's so good to hear your voice. I've missed you so much."

The words broke the barrier around her heart, releasing a flood of emotions. "I'm sorry, Mom. I've missed you, too."

Gil poured a second cup of coffee and carried it into the family room. He rarely had time for more than a gulp each morning. Today he relished the extra time. His gaze fixed on the backyard beyond the French doors. Spring would be here soon. He was ready. The off-and-on cold weather dampened his mood. He preferred warm weather any day. He looked forward to watching Abby play on the swing. Maybe he'd build her a playhouse if she wasn't too old for that kind of thing. So much he wanted to do for her, so much to make up for.

The back door swooshed opened, which meant Julie was probably here. He met her in the kitchen.

"You're still here? Is everything all right? Abby okay?"

He held up a hand to forestall her concerns. "Everything is fine. I'm going to a job site this morning and I don't need to be there until nine."

"Oh. Good. I was worried."

Something in her tone caught his attention. Her usual smile was missing, her brown eyes lacked the sparkle that he found so appealing. "Now it's my turn to ask. Is everything okay?"

"Sure."

Gil tilted his head. "I know a fake smile when I see one."

She moved away, going to the coffeemaker and pouring a cup. "I'm just tired. I didn't sleep well last night."

"Want to talk about it?"

"Not really. It's just family stuff."

He joined her at the counter, resting his hip against the edge. "I've never heard you talk about your family. Why is that?"

"We're not close. I haven't seen them in years."

He held her gaze, waiting for further explanation. She resisted but finally exhaled a small sigh.

"I have an older sister. She was a competitive diver. She had an accident during practice one day that left her paralyzed from the neck down. She needed round-the-clock care. It changed my family. Maryann took all their time and money and attention."

"And you were shoved aside."

She lowered her eyes and nodded. "I understood. I knew my sister needed them more than I did, but I realized I needed to strike out on my own. They had their hands full. So I went off to college, and we drifted apart."

He touched her cheek. "I'm sorry. You must have felt abandoned."

"At times, but I've managed." Gil pulled her into his arms. She didn't resist. He knew she needed comfort right now. She rested her head on his chest, and he felt her relax against him.

"But when someone you love shuts you out of their lives, it's hard to come to terms with. Leah started pulling away long before she left me. I tried everything to make her happy, but it was never enough. Abby wasn't enough. I wasn't enough. She walked out as if I didn't matter."

"I know. That's how I felt, too. Thankfully I met DiDi and she's become my best friend, my lifeline. I don't think I'd have survived without her."

"For me it was my parents. I wish they were home now. I could use their advice and support. Which is ironic since the one time I ignored my father's advice, and my attorney's, it led to the mess I'm in now."

"What do you mean?"

"He told me not to give Leah full custody of Abby. My lawyer warned me that I could lose all access to her. But Leah assured me I could see her anytime. I thought I was doing what was best for Abby. But it only made things worse." Julie stepped out of his arms, leaving a chill on his skin. But the tenderness in her eyes when she looked at him quickly warmed him again.

"No. From what I've learned about bipolar disorder, nothing you could have done would have changed anything. You shouldn't blame yourself for things you can't control."

"What about things we can control? Like the way we feel?" He took her arms in his hands and drew her close again. "The way people can change our perspective on things, make us look at life differently." He placed his palm against the side of her face. His pulse raced as he saw her reaction. She'd come into his life and changed everything for the better. He couldn't deny being drawn to her.

She met his gaze, looking deep into his eyes, and stirring feelings he'd long ignored. She placed her small hand over his.

"Gil, I think—"

"I'm ready, Miss Julie."

Gil dropped his hands and quickly picked up his coffee cup. He'd forgotten Abby was still in the house. He'd have to be more careful. He tended to lose his train of thought when Julie was close.

Julie grabbed her purse and tugged the car keys from the front pocket. "We'd better get moving. Don't want to be late for school."

Abby gave him a quick hug, patted Ruffles's head then scooped up her backpack on the way out the door. Julie caught his gaze before she pulled the door closed. Her brown eyes held understanding. They'd found mutual ground. Maybe sharing their feelings would help them both move forward.

But forward for him meant staying in Dover. Forward for Julie meant moving to Paris. His good mood sank.

Julie's eyes filled with tears of joy as she looked at her little princess Thursday afternoon. Abby stood awkwardly on the platform as the seamstress, Mrs. Fodor, finished pinning up the hem of the pale lavender and white dress she wore. "You look beautiful, Abby. Like a real princess." Abby smiled but fidgeted, earning a calm reminder from the seamstress to remain still so she wouldn't be stuck with a pin. "It was nice of your aunt Gemma to invite you to be part of the wedding." Abby had been reluctant to participate, but they'd been practicing walking and tossing fake petals and now she was looking forward to it. Having Evan to walk with helped.

Abby nodded, holding the skirt out to admire the

frilly fabric. "I'm glad she picked a purple dress for me to wear."

"Me, too. It's a perfect color with your dark hair."

Mrs. Fodor stood and stepped back. "All done. I'll have the alterations ready by the end of the week. You can stop by Friday." The woman removed the yellow measuring tape from around her neck. "She'll be an adorable flower girl. I've enjoyed working on this wedding. After what Gemma did with our Christmas celebrations, the whole town loves her. And she's marrying one of our favorite sons."

Julie handed Abby her coat and helped her slip it on. "The Montgomerys are much admired. I'm looking forward to meeting all of them." Julie thanked the seamstress again, then said goodbye. Cold wind assaulted them as they stepped outside. The week of nice weather was gone, pushed aside by a cold front bringing rain and chilly temperatures. Typical Mississippi weather.

She took Abby's hand. "As soon as we buy a chew toy for Ruffles, we'll go home and fix some popcorn and watch a movie. Which one should we watch today?"

"Annie."

Purchase completed, they hurried back down the block toward the car. The wind had picked up, and Julie quickened her pace. Abby stopped in her tracks, jerking Julie to a halt. She looked at the little girl, her heart thudding in her chest at the look of terror on her child's face. "Abby? Sweetie, what's wrong?"

Julie turned in the direction of Abby's gaze, but saw nothing but shoppers and cars passing by.

Tears spilled down her cheeks. "I thought I saw my aunt."

"Gemma?"

She shook her head. "Aunt Pam." She threw her arms around Julie and held on for dear life. "Please don't make me go back with her. I want to stay with Daddy."

"You will, sweetie. Your daddy won't let you go away ever again."

Abby sniffled. "Are you sure?"

Julie squeezed her hand. "I am." Abby started to shake, her little face pale and scrunched up as she began to cry harder. Julie searched for a way to reassure her. "In fact, why don't we go see him right now and he can tell you himself."

"He's at work."

"I know, but I don't think he'll mind if you visit. I've never seen where your daddy works, have you?"

Abby stared out the window of the car as Julie followed her GPS directions to Montgomery Electrical. She'd stopped crying but withdrew into silence. Julie prayed that Gil would be able to reassure her and ease her fears.

Pulling into the parking lot, Julie was surprised at the size of the building. The two-story brick facade gave the impression of a solid, respectable business. Extending behind was a large metal-roofed structure she guessed was the warehouse. The parking area to the side was filled with a variety of pickups, vans and bucket trucks.

Julie held Abby's hand as they entered the building. Only then did it occur to her she should have called first. Their sudden appearance might alarm Gil.

A young woman in jeans and a knit top sat behind a small reception desk. "I'm Julie Bishop, and this is

Abby, Gil Montgomery's daughter. We need to see him right away."

The woman made a quick call before smiling and directing them toward the stairs. "He'll be waiting."

Abby held tight to Julie's hand. She prayed that Gil could ease the child's fears because her eyes were still big as saucers, and her hands clammy. She needed the reassuring presence of her daddy. And she knew Gil wouldn't disappoint.

Chapter Eight

Gil stopped at the top of the stairs, his mind flashing through all the reasons why Julie would bring Abby to the shop. None of them good. One glance at his daughter's face as she topped the stairs and his heart seized. He looked at Julie for an explanation. "What's going on?"

"Abby needed to see you." Julie released Abby's hand, and she came to him, wrapping her arms around his waist. The gesture shot his concern a level higher.

Inside Gil's office he led his daughter to the small seating area in the corner and pulled her down beside him on the sofa. "What's wrong? Are you hurt?"

Abby looked up at him, her brown eyes troubled and her lower lip puckered out. "I saw my aunt."

"You mean Gemma?"

"No. Aunt Pam. She was in the park. I don't want to go back with her. Don't make me go. I want to stay with you."

He hugged her to his side. "Of course you're stay-ing here. I won't ever let you go away. Are you sure it was Aunt Pam? Maybe it was just someone who looked like her."

"No. It was her. I know." Abby laid her head on his chest and cried. Julie handed her tissues from her purse.

He glanced at Julie, her expression contorted in concern. "It's all right, Abby. Even if she is here, she can't take you back with her. She's not allowed. You're going to stay here with me and Miss Julie."

Reassured by his words, Abby stopped crying. She wiped her cheeks and glanced around the office.

Julie cleared her throat. "Gil, Abby has never been here before. Maybe she'd like to see what you do when you're at work."

He frowned, puzzled at her suggestion. She raised her eyebrows and stared pointedly back at him. She was trying to distract Abby and give her something else to think about. "Oh, sure. Would you like that, sweet pea?" She nodded and sniffled.

Julie drew him aside as Abby began to wander around the office. "Do you think she really saw your sister-in-law?"

He rubbed his forehead. "I don't know. Maybe. But she knows I have a restraining order. Though I wouldn't put it past her. She's a very manipulative woman."

Abby held up a framed photo on his desk. "That's you and that's Grandma."

Gil pointed out his dad and his siblings, then he picked up a picture of Abby when she was smaller. "Guess who this is."

Abby smiled as she took the frame in her hand. "It's me."

"That's right." He picked up the other frame. "And

here's one of you and Ruffles. I keep it here so I can look at you when I miss you."

"Can I have a picture of you to keep in my room?"

Such a simple request, but it took him a moment to find his voice. "Of course."

Julie dug into her purse. "Let's take one right now to remember your first visit to your daddy's office." She activated the camera on her smartphone. "Stand in front of the desk and smile."

Gil's insides melted into a gooey lump. Why hadn't he thought of this sooner? Julie took several shots, then handed them the phone. The images displayed a sight he never thought he'd see. Him and his little girl together smiling. He looked at Julie to thank her and saw her brown eyes peering at him, as if she was trying to convey a message.

"I have some personal matters to take care of. Why don't you and Abby spend some time together? Maybe go for pizza, or a burger? I'll see you at home."

It was a good idea. One he should have thought of himself. For reasons he didn't understand, she'd made it her mission to ensure he and his daughter were close. He became more indebted to her each day. Without her wisdom and insight, he might still be dealing with a child who retreated to her room instead of enjoying impromptu father-daughter time. She was showing him how to be a father to his little girl.

He grinned at Abby. "What do you say, sweet pea? Does that sound like fun?" Her wide, happy grin solidified the idea.

Julie waved goodbye and slipped out.

Gil watched as Abby wandered around his office, examining everything she saw. "I'm starving. How about after we tour the shop, we go to Angelo's World Famous Pizza for supper? I'll show you how to play the games in the back."

With a wide smile and a skip, she hurried toward him and took his hand, filling him with so much joy he almost believed he could fly to Angelo's on happiness alone. He'd never looked forward to pizza so much in his life.

Julie scanned the list of acts for the talent show one more time. The event had been so popular that she'd had to schedule an intermission to get them all in. As reluctant as she'd been to take on this project, she was enjoying working with those involved. Nancy Scott had proved to be a phenomenal organizer. Jim Barrett, pastor of Peace Community, had become the head cheerleader for the event, coming up with new ideas every day on how to promote it. She and Nancy had to stop him. They were near to filling up the VFW hall as it was, and there wasn't another place in Dover large enough to hold the event.

Her gaze drifted to the two guitars in the corner of the family room. One regular size, one half-size. Gil had decided to open with "Jesus Loves Me." He'd found additional verses they could sing. They were also singing "This Little Light of Mine." Watching the two of them practice, Gil patiently showing Abby the chords and placing her little fingers on the strings, never failed to warm her heart and bring tears to her eyes.

For all her guilt in keeping the truth from them, she wouldn't trade this time for anything. She'd have warm and beautiful memories to take with her to Paris in a few weeks. But her heart, that would remain behind.

She'd given it to Abby the day she was born and, despite her best efforts not to, she'd lost her heart to Gil, too. The attraction between them was growing. She knew he had feelings for her, but she'd rebuffed every one. That one brief kiss the other day had shown her how vulnerable she was to his charm, and she could not succumb to her feelings, no matter how strong.

A glance at the clock reminded her that it was almost time to pick up Abby. She cherished their moments together, and Abby seemed more inclined to talk on the way home. She and Hannah had become best friends, and Julie found endless amusement in the crazy things they wanted to do together. Going to see the upcoming princess movie she could handle. Taking a field trip to the rain forest to find fairies was something else again.

A knock sounded on the kitchen door. It had been a couple of days since Nancy had delivered a cake, pie or cookies. The sumptuous desserts were tightening the waist of her jeans. She opened the door with a smile, but a stranger stood on the low stoop. Something in the icy blue eyes triggered her concern. "May I help you?"

"I've come to see Abigail. I'm her aunt Pam."

A shiver chased down Julie's spine. Her impulse was to slam the door in her face. But the woman was a relative of Abby's. She couldn't ignore that. "I'm sorry. Abby's not here. Perhaps you could come back this evening when her father is here."

"Where is she? I have a right to see her!"

There was no way she would give the woman any information. Waves of antagonism washed toward her from the woman, strengthening her resolve. "She's not home." The woman's eyes narrowed, staring at her intensely, scanning her face. Her eyes widened, and a sly, knowing smile appeared on her thin lips. Alarmed, Julie grabbed her keys and purse from the table beside the door. "I'm sorry, but I have an appointment. You'll have to excuse me." She locked the door, pulling it shut behind her as she stepped out, forcing the woman to back off the stoop and onto the driveway. "It might be best if you checked with Mr. Montgomery before returning."

The woman raised her chin, a sly smirk on her narrow face. "I'll do that."

Julie hurried to the car, her hands shaking. She longed to call Gil, but first she wanted to put as much distance as possible between herself and Abby's aunt Pam. She took a circuitous route to the school in case the woman tried to follow her. As soon as she was in the pickup line at the school, she pulled out her phone and called Gil.

"I really thought Abby was mistaken about seeing her. I wanted to think it was a look-alike that triggered her memory. I never thought she'd come here."

"Maybe all she wants is to see Abby."

"Maybe, but I know this woman. She'll stop at nothing to get her way. I discovered she was the source of a lot of the troubles in my marriage. Pam used Leah's illness to twist everything."

"Why would she do that?"

"Pam raised Leah from the time she was twelve. She sees herself as Leah's mother. She's always been overly involved with her life. "

Julie struggled to swallow past the tightness in her throat. "Gil, what if she comes back?" She hated that she sounded like a scared little kid, but something about the woman had rattled her. That knowing smile could mean only one thing. She'd noticed the resemblance between her and Abby. How long before she shared that observation with Gil?

"You and Abby go shopping or something. I'll get away as soon as I can. I'll text you when I'm home."

"You don't think she'll do anything crazy, do you?"

"No. She's not dangerous, only possessive. I knew she'd want to see Abby eventually, just not this soon. Don't worry. I'll fix this."

Julie navigated the weekend traffic through downtown Dover on her way to the VFW hall. Gil and Abby's time together yesterday had gone well. Abby talked about the trucks that went up in the air, how her daddy's office was bigger than Uncle Linc's and the games she and her dad had played in the pizza restaurant's fun room. It was clear both had enjoyed their time together. Gil was much more relaxed than she'd ever seen him. Abby had bugged her dad until he printed out the photo of them from the office and made Julie promise to go shopping for a special frame soon.

Nothing had been heard from Aunt Pam. Gil assured her that Pam had returned to Mobile and he had everything under control if she showed up again.

Thankfully, Julie had preparations for the talent show to occupy her mind. She'd spent most of the morning with Nancy and the committee going over logistics. Julie pulled up at the sprawling VFW hall. Gil was installing the extra electrical power needed to support the lights and sound for the show today. Inside she followed the noises to the back of the building. The air smelled like fresh paint and cleaning materials. It was amazing how the members had taken ownership of the event and jumped in to make the place sparkle. "Gil?"

"Back here."

She turned at the first open door to find him in front of a large metal box with a pair of pliers in his hand.

"What are you doing here?" His surprised look slid quickly into a warm smile of delight, triggering a sudden bump in her pulse.

She held up the bag from Fil-Er-Up Burgers. She'd discovered the quaint burger joint housed in a repurposed old filling station and couldn't get enough of the homemade fries. "When you texted that work was going slowly, I thought I'd bring you something to keep you going."

"Thanks. It smells good. Where's Abby?"

"She's spending the day with Hannah. They are watching movies together."

He slipped the pliers into the tool belt fastened around his lean hips. "Let's go to the kitchen. I could use some time off my feet."

They settled at one of the small metal tables. "Thanks for thinking of me."

"Nannies are trained to think of everyone in the family."

He raised his eyebrows. "So, you're saying you didn't do it because I'm special?"

"Nope. You're just another one of my kiddos."

He held her gaze. "I don't believe you. From what I've seen, all your kiddos are special. Even the grown-up ones."

She blushed. "Eat. You have more work to do and the dinner is right around the corner. It's looking wonderful in here."

"Yeah. All it needs is the decorations."

She thought about the exposed wires and the boxes on the floor that held electrical equipment. "This must be costing you a lot, Gil. Not to mention the time. Why didn't you have some of your employees do the job?"

"Employees cost money. The boss works for free. As for the materials, we have a whole warehouse full of equipment. Besides, it was time I got my hands dirty again. I've been in the office too long." He shrugged. "These men of the VFW have given to their country and to their community. Now it's my turn. A chance to help my church and my town."

"You're a good man, Gilbreth Montgomery."

He stopped midbite, lowered his burger to the table and groaned softly. "Who told you my real name?"

"No one. I get the mail each day, remember? One of the bills had your full name on it."

"I try to keep that name off the radar."

Julie giggled and popped a fry into her mouth. "Let me guess, it was your mother's maiden name."

Gil nodded, his expression pained. "Right. Good old Southern tradition."

"Don't feel so bad. My middle name is my mother's maiden name, too."

He twisted his expression into an evil glare. "I hope it's something really awful."

"Joyce. Her maiden name was Joyce. I'm Julianna Joyce Bishop."

Gil grimaced. "That's not even fair."

Julie couldn't stop the laughter bubbling up from inside. "Sorry. Are your brothers and sisters all named for family members?"

"How'd you guess? Grandparents, favorite uncles

and aunts, grandmothers. I have to admit I didn't resist when Leah wanted to name our baby Abigail. As far as I know there are no other Abigails on the family tree."

"Does your mother know you hate your name?"

"Oh, yeah. But she just reminds me what a noble family name it is."

"I'm looking forward to meeting your mother."

"I think she'd like you." Gil balled up the sandwich wrapper and stood, taking his drink. "I better get back to work."

Julie stood. "Go. I'll clean up. How much more do you have to do?"

"Another hour or so."

"I'm going to stay a few minutes. I want to take measurements of the stage."

"Thanks for the lunch." He held her gaze a long moment, then walked away, leaving a warm tingle deep inside her middle. She watched him disappear around the corner, unable to keep from admiring his masculine stride and the confident sway of his shoulders. She wanted to know more about him. Everything. A dangerous sign that she was in over her head. Her feelings for Gil would have to remain her secret. A dream that would remain unfulfilled.

Julie took her measurements, sketched a layout on her tablet then prepared to leave the building. She was halfway to the door when she heard a loud pop and a shout. "Gil?"

Heart pounding, she hurried through the building to the back hall where he'd been working. He was seated awkwardly on the floor, holding his hand and grimacing in pain. She ran to him and stooped down. "Are you all right?"

He nodded, gritting his teeth. "Stupid mistake. Guess I've been away from this too long."

He started to stand, and she slipped her arm around his waist for support. Not that she could do much. He was a solid mass of muscle. "Let me see your hand." Other than a red patch, she didn't see any other damage.

"I'll be fine, but this'll sting for a couple days."

She took his hand, examining the skin gently with her fingertips, acutely aware of his warmth. "Are you sure you're okay? When I heard you shout, I thought you'd been electrocuted."

He stared into her eyes. "No. I just took a nasty shock. It's a hazard of the trade. But I'm glad you were worried."

"Of course I was. I care about you."

"Because you like me, or because I'm Abby's father?"

"Both." Standing close to him, the all-male mixture of warm flannel shirt, oil and leather from the tool belt went to her head. Why did he always smell so good? He shifted and slipped his arms around her waist, tugging her close. She avoided looking at him. "You need to be more careful."

"Because?"

"Abby needs you."

"What do you need, Julie?"

"Gil, you know I'm leaving soon. We shouldn't."

"That's why we should. We only have this short time together. Shouldn't we make a memory to carry us through the rest of our lives?"

"Is that one of your pickup lines?"

Gil chuckled. "I've been off the market for a long

time, Julie. I'm a one-woman man. I don't have flirting skills." He slid his hand along her jaw, his thumb gently rubbing her cheek. "All I know is that I like being with you. I like having you in my home. I like having you in my life, and I think you like being here."

His touch was fogging her thoughts and turning her insides into warm mush. "I do. I wish I could stay. But my future is overseas." Gil lowered his hand and stepped back, a wry smile softening his features.

"I think that's one of the things I like about you most, Julie. You don't play games, you speak your mind. You're always honest."

The cold rush of reality chilled her veins and drained the blood from her head so fast she thought she might pass out. "What?"

"After living so many years with lies and manipulation, it's nice to have someone in my life who's an open book." He touched the tip of her nose, then gently steered her toward the door. "Go. Being here alone with you is not a good idea."

Julie nodded, unable to speak. He had no idea how bad an idea it actually was.

Julie checked over Abby's math assignment, smiling as she slid the paper back across the table. "Good job, Abby. I think you're almost caught up. Maybe we can stop the extra lessons soon."

"Good. 'Cause I still don't like math. But it's not as yucky as it used to be."

She laughed at the intensity of her child's comment. "That's good to hear."

"I'm going to practice my guitar."

She remained at the table, sorting through her trou-

bled thoughts. Gil thought she was honest. The sharp
edges of her conscience plowed across her heart. She'd
driven up to Jackson yesterday to attend church with
DiDi, and the sermon about putting off falsehood and
speaking truthfully had pierced her to the core.

Gil thought she was honest and truthful, when she
was actually no better than his ex-wife, hiding her real
reason for being in his home and her real relationship.
Thankfully, in a few weeks her assignment would be
over. She'd be at peace with Abby's future, and she
could arrive in Paris ready to start a whole new life.

Who was she kidding? She might be moving to
the city of her dreams, but her heart would remain in
Dover. Forever.

Until then, she'd add as many memories to her mental catalog as she could. Moving to the family room,
she curled up on the couch, chuckling as Ruffles raised
her front paws against Abby's guitar as she tried to
strum the strings.

"No, Ruffles. Down. You'll scratch it, and then I
won't be able to play with Daddy."

"Ruffles, come." The pup whirled, wagged its tail
then vaulted into her lap, wiggling and attempting to
lick her face. The obedience classes had been helpful,
but Ruffles was still a puppy at heart and until she got a
little older, she was unpredictable. But Julie would miss
the playful exuberance the little dog displayed now.

The knock on the back door shattered her good
mood, knotting her stomach. Had the aunt come back
to demand to see Abby? Gil had given her strict in-
structions to call the police if she showed up again.
Stomach swirling, she stood and went to the door. The
woman outside the window wasn't Pam. She was older

with gray hair, a trim figure and a pleasant friendly face. She opened the door and noticed the cobalt blue eyes. The same as Gil's.

The woman's smile widened. "You must be Julie. I'm Francie Montgomery. Gil's mother."

Relief whooshed out in a quick breath. "Hello. Please, come in. I'm so glad to meet you, Mrs. Montgomery."

Francie stepped into the kitchen and glanced around. "Please call me Francie. Something smells good. Gil told me you had started cooking evening meals." She met Julie's gaze. "He's enjoying coming home to a nice dinner."

Did Gil talk about her to his mother? "Oh, well, that's nice. I enjoy cooking for them."

Ruffles loped into the kitchen and sat at Francie's feet, bushy tail wagging. "You must be the new member of the family. What a cutie." She scooped up the pup and held her close. "I'm glad to see you, too, but I really came to see my granddaughter."

"Oh, of course. She's in the family room practicing. I had no idea you'd come home."

Francie met her gaze again. "I asked Gil not to tell you I was coming. First impressions can be important, don't you think?"

A twinge of discomfort touched her nerves. "Yes. I do." Was Francie trying to imply something with her comment? Probably not. Merely her guilty conscience at work. Julie followed Francie into the family room. "Abby, look who's here to see you."

Abby glanced up and smiled. "Hi, Grandma. You came back."

"I did. Did you miss me?" Abby set her guitar aside and came into her grandmother's arms.

Julie's heart warmed at the sight. Francie exuded warmth and caring. It was easy to see why she'd made a connection with Abby so quickly. On the heels of that thought came the realization that with Francie back in Dover, her job as nanny was at an end. Her throat compressed. It was for the best considering her precarious situation, but she wasn't ready to leave. She wasn't sure if she'd ever be ready.

"And I taught her a few tricks. Do you want to see them?"

"Of course." Francie glanced over her shoulder at Julie. "Excuse me while I admire the accomplishments of my grand-dog."

She watched through the window as Abby put Ruffles through her paces in the backyard. Since it was a chilly day, Julie put on the kettle in case Francie wanted a cup of tea. She'd seen several packages of loose tea in the cupboard and assumed Francie had kept them there, since she'd never seen Gil drink anything but sweet tea and coffee.

Chilly air accompanied Francie and Abby as they came into the house. Francie joined Julie in the kitchen. "That is one cute puppy Abby has lost her heart to. Gil tells me that was your idea, too."

"Oh, not really. Abby told me she'd had a dog once, and I thought it might help her feel more at home here. Would you like a cup of tea?"

"That would be nice."

Julie carried the tea set to the table and joined Francie, her probing blue gaze a match to her son's.

"I appreciate you convincing my son to enter the

talent show with Abby. It's been too long since he's picked up his guitar. I think all he's been through in the last six months stole much of his joy. Sharing his love of music with Abby should help them draw closer."

"That's what I was hoping." Uncomfortable with the topic, Julie attempted to change the conversation. "Gil told me about your daughter's accident. How's she doing? I thought you'd be in London longer."

Francie set her cup in the saucer with a shake of her head. "She is bullheaded and determined. Just like her father. We flew back to New York last weekend. She decided to stay and work with a physical therapist who specializes in dancer's injuries. Though I'm not sure it will change anything. I'm afraid her professional career is over."

"That's too bad."

"It breaks my heart. It's all she ever wanted to do since she was five years old. I honestly don't know how she's going to cope with losing her dream. I'm praying the Lord will open up some new opportunities for her, but she'll resist with everything she has. It runs in the family. Once my children set their mind to something, they don't change easily."

"I've noticed that trait in your son. Gil has never wavered in his desire to reconnect with Abby."

"He's been lost without her. It's such a blessing to have her here with us."

Julie cleared her throat. Might as well get to the heart of her concerns. "Now that you're back, I'm sure you're eager to start taking care of Abby again."

"Actually, I was hoping you'd stay on for a few more weeks. You're doing a wonderful job here. You obviously care a great deal about my son and granddaughter, and they like you. I see no reason to mess with a good thing. Besides, I'll be going back to New York in a few weeks."

"Oh?" Julie hoped her immense relief wasn't visible on her face.

Francie nodded. "That's about how long it'll take for Bethany to figure out she can't bury her head in the sand any longer, and she'll need me to help her move back home." She paused and stared at her teacup a long moment. "It's the hard part of being a mother."

Julie pressed her lips together. Leaving her family had taught her self-reliance and courage. "Sometimes, failing is the only way to learn the lessons of life."

Francie met her gaze. "That's what I told Gil. He was too quick to protect Abby from any bumps and bruises."

"I think he was afraid of pushing her further away."

"I agree, but you've helped him get past that. You're a very wise woman for one so young."

"Not really. I just have a lot of experience with children."

"Which is fortunate for my granddaughter. I volunteered to help in the kitchen so I could be there to see the talent show this weekend. I wish Dale could have been here to see it. He'd be so happy to know Abby is home again."

"I was sorry to hear about your husband."

"Thank you. It's been a difficult time for the family. The children adored their father. Gil suffered multiple losses. I worried that he would never be himself again. Of course, none of this would have happened if Leah had been truthful with him from the start about her illness."

Julie's throat burned. Did Francie know about her deception? Impossible. For some reason she felt compelled to reply. "Maybe she felt ashamed. Maybe she feared he wouldn't love her if he'd known the truth."

"If she loved him, she should have trusted him. I know my son, and he would have stayed by her side no matter what. He's devoted to those he loves. Secrets never serve a purpose. Don't you agree?"

Something in Francie's penetrating gaze pricked her conscience. It was as if she was speaking on a different level. But how could that be? A cheery sound came from her phone, alerting her to a text message from the director of the International School. "Excuse me for a moment. This message is from overseas."

She slipped away from the table and read the text. They were asking if she could come to Paris a few weeks early. Julie bit her bottom lip. This could be her out. A way to extricate herself from the Montgomerys without creating any hurt feelings. But the thought of leaving Gil and Abby before she was ready twisted her heart in knots. She tapped a quick, noncommittal response and returned to the table. "Sorry. The school I'll be working at in Paris would like me to come a few weeks early."

"Oh, yes. Gil told me you would be moving overseas. So will you be leaving soon?"

"I'll have to think about it. I'm not sure."

Francie tilted her head and studied her. "Because you found something here you don't want to leave behind?"

Julie met her gaze, and the knowing look in Francie's eyes sent a chill down her spine. Julie knew without a doubt that Francie had guessed the relationship between her and Abby was much more than nanny and child. Before she could comment, Francie stood and called to Abby.

"Come give me a hug, Abby." She faced Julie. "I'd better go. I promised my soon-to-be daughter-in-law that I would give her my opinion on the wedding cake."

After getting a warm hug from Abby, Francie said goodbye. Abby asked to go to Hannah's to play, and Julie quickly gave permission, eager for some time alone. She couldn't shake the feeling Francie had somehow discovered the truth. Was her secret written on her face? Of course it was. Abby looked like her. Anyone could see that.

Nancy had commented about the resemblance once. Pam's expression said she knew, and now Francie. A swell of anxiety mushroomed up through her body, compressing her lungs, increasing her heart rate. How much longer could she hide the truth? She couldn't believe Gil hadn't seen it for himself. What would happen when he did? What about Abby? Ruffles licked her ankle, and she reached down and scooped up the puppy, taking comfort from the warm furry body. *Lord, I don't know what to do. I can't go and I can't stay. Help me find a way that won't hurt the ones I love.*

She doubted such a way existed. And she had only herself to blame.

Chapter Nine

The VFW hall was buzzing with activity Saturday morning when Julie arrived. The kitchen was full of cooks already infusing the air with wonderful smells. Tables and chairs were being put up in the main area and the stage was being decorated with potted plants and a hand-painted backdrop created by a member of the church. She checked her list again, making final adjustments. Two acts had withdrawn. Ed and Becky Zimmerman due to a case of flu, and Jeff Easton and his granddaughter because of stage fright. Thankfully it wouldn't impact the lineup too much, and the shortened schedule would be welcome. She'd been afraid the show was running too long.

Veteran Arthur Coker was busy working with the wires and microphones needed on the stage. This was the first chance she'd had to see the newly donated sound system, and the sight of it stopped her in her tracks. It was huge, taking up a large space along the wall. "Art, will this thing be ready for this afternoon? I'd like to run a sound check before dress rehearsal."

"No problem." He straightened his rail-thin body

and flashed a smile that made his dark eyes twinkle even more than usual. "It's a sweet system. Shouldn't have any trouble hearing anyone with this baby."

Julie smiled and nodded, but inside she was worried. The speakers looked as if they could blast the entire audience through the roof. She scolded herself for her ungrateful attitude. The system had been donated by the owner of the local hardware store.

Nancy strolled by and stopped at her side. "Quite a blessing, isn't it?"

"More than I'd expected from a hardware store."

"Oh, that didn't come from the store. Adam Holbrook, Tom Durrant's son-in-law, had that sent from his family company in Atlanta."

"It's very generous of him."

"He jumped right in when he heard about the old system not being big enough to handle the show."

She brushed off her concerns. In her short time in Dover, she'd come to accept that people here were quick to lend their hands and their resources to help. She'd have to trust that the others would do their job. She had enough on her plate.

Dress rehearsal began on time. Jacob Kelly's duet with his daughter, Anna, was the lead act. They took the stage and lifted their microphones from the stand. But as they started to sing, a loud screech filled the air and the lights went out in the building.

Julie's heart sank. There wasn't time for any complications. The dinner started in a few hours. The kitchen needed power to prepare the meals. She went in search of Art, who was fiddling with the new sound equipment.

His thick brows were pulled together in a deep

frown. "I think you'd better put a call in to the Montgomery boys. This new system has too much power for our wiring."

"But Gil just rewired the entire building."

"I know, but he hadn't counted on this top-of-the-line gadgetry."

She made a quick call to Gil, who assured her he and Linc would be right over. Half an hour later she found them in the back hall pulling wires and hooking up another metal box.

"How long will this take?"

"Almost done." He flashed a smile over his shoulder.

She exhaled a sigh of relief and rested a hand on his arm. "You're my hero."

Linc coughed loudly. "So does that make me Robin to his Batman?"

She grinned. "You're heroic, too. Thank you."

Thankfully no additional glitches occurred. The dress rehearsal went smoothly, and the sound system worked perfectly. Satisfied all was in order, Julie slipped away to get ready for the evening, returning to the hall as guests were arriving for the dinner. She stepped into the kitchen and saw Francie at the counter waving at her.

"How are my guitar players doing? Is Abby nervous about tonight?"

"She was. We could hardly hear her singing in rehearsal, but we adjusted the microphone and I think she'll be okay."

"I have to admit I'm anxious about it. She's so shy."

"I know, but Gil has been bolstering her confidence. As long as he's there, she should be fine."

Before she knew it the dinner was almost over and

the acts were lining up. She handled a few unexpected changes, shuffled some props and laughed at a couple of humorous onstage mishaps, but so far each act had been delightful. No matter what the talent, seeing fathers and daughters together warmed hearts. Now it was Gil and Abby's turn.

They took the stage in their matching lavender checked shirts—something Gil wasn't thrilled with, but he'd graciously accepted his daughter's choice. They took their seats onstage, both carrying their guitar. Julie tried to quell the nervous bubbling in her stomach. She noticed that Gil had rearranged their positions since the rehearsal. Both chairs were angled toward each other and not facing front. Gil leaned close to Abby and whispered in her ear. She nodded and positioned her little guitar. Gil strummed the first chord, then they began to sing. Abby kept her eyes either on her guitar strings or on her father. She sang out loud and sweet. The combination of Gil's rich baritone and Abby's sweet child's soprano was poignant. Tears filled her eyes, her heart swelled, pressing painfully against her ribs. Never had she been so proud of anything in her life. Watching Gil and Abby was the most beautiful sight she'd ever seen.

"Thank you."

Julie heard Francie whisper into her ear, but she was too emotional to respond and could only nod.

"You'll never know what this means to me and to my son."

The rest of the show went on without a hitch. The judges, Pastor Jim Barrett, choir director, April Craig, and the youth minster, Jake Langford, took the stage to announce the winners. Third place went to Steve and

Bonnie Mullins for their juggling act. Second place went to Gil and Abby. Willie Burns and his daughter Candy took first place for their tap dance.

Abby beamed with delight when she accepted the small trophy. They took their bows, then hurried off the stage and came directly to her. Gil grinned like a little boy. "How about that? Second place."

Abby gave Julie a hug, then one to her grandmother. "We got a prize."

Francie pulled out her smartphone and swiped it. "I want a picture of this moment." She motioned father and child together. They gripped their guitars, the genuine plastic trophy held proudly between them.

Julie fought back tears. Her simple idea to enter the talent show had reaped more rewards than she'd ever imagined.

Francie motioned her forward. "Come get into this picture."

Her throat tightened. She couldn't be photographed with Abby. She might as well put up a billboard announcing the truth to the whole town.

"No. That's sweet, but I don't photograph well. I really need to make sure everything is under control backstage. I'll see y'all later. I might be late. There's a lot of tearing down to do."

She tried to ignore the look of disappointment on Gil's and Abby's faces and the knowing glance Francie had given her. Every day her secret became harder to bear. She consoled herself with the thought that this was Gil and Abby's moment. She said goodbye and turned to go, only to have Gil take her arm and pull her aside.

"Julie, what is it? I thought you'd be thrilled that we

won a prize. None of this would have happened without you. Why don't you come and celebrate with us? We're taking Abby for ice cream."

"That's nice, but I can't leave until things here are all cleared away. I promised Nancy." He searched her face as if looking for an explanation. His confusion softened her heart, and she reached up and touched his face. "I'm so proud of you and Abby. It was the sweetest act all night. It was a good idea to shift the chairs so she could see you. You're a wonderful father, Gil."

His brows drew together in a frown. "It's because of you. All of this."

Her heart squeezed. "No. All I did was suggest. You made it happen." She stepped back. "I have to go. Enjoy your ice cream."

Turning her attention to the hall, she let the chatter of well-wishers and performers divert her thoughts from Gil and Abby. The VFW members had assured her they would dismantle things, and the church women had already cleaned the kitchen. But Julie remained until the last guest and contestant had departed.

Thankfully Gil's car wasn't in the driveway when she arrived home. Hurrying into her apartment, she kept the lights off as she prepared for bed. She needed the darkness and the silence to think. She'd made a disturbing discovery this evening. She was in love with Gil. Somewhere she'd stepped over the line and hadn't realized it until she watched him and Abby onstage. She'd fought it from the start because it was reckless, and impossible and wrong. But she'd lost the battle. Now she had to rebuild her barriers and keep her distance before she made a fool of herself. Gil couldn't know.

She hadn't yet responded to the request to go to Paris early. Maybe now was the time to decide.

Sunday afternoon was warm and sunny, and all Julie wanted to do was hide in her apartment and watch a movie. But she'd been invited to a party, and there was no way out. The Montgomerys were celebrating Gil and Abby's talent show award and welcoming their mother back home.

Picking up her purse, she locked her door and started down the stairs. Gil was waiting beside his car and graciously opened the door for her. Julie tried to quell the anxiety in her chest. Abby had gone home with Francie after church to help, which left Julie to ride alone with Gil. "Are you sure I should come to this party? I'm not family."

Gil winked. "No, but you're a close friend, and Abby would be crushed if you missed it. Besides, my mother told me not to show up without you."

"I like your mother." Despite her concerns about what Francie might have figured out, she enjoyed being around the woman.

"She's impossible not to like."

Julie focused her attention to the landscape outside the car window. The city street gave way to a two-lane road lined with trees and newly plowed fields. The car slowed and made a left turn into a winding tree-covered driveway.

She'd never given much thought to where Gil's family lived, but the sight of the large home as they emerged from the trees roused her curiosity. The three-story mansion was a pleasing combination of late Victorian and Greek revival, nestled in the middle of a lush lawn surrounded by hundred-year-old live oaks. Yet despite its majestic appearance, there was something welcoming about the stately home.

The interior confirmed her first impression. The home was cozy, comfortable and unpretentious. A family home. It made sense. Francie wasn't a pretentious woman. She wouldn't be comfortable in a perfectly decorated home.

Her tension eased as she entered the kitchen and received a warm welcome from Francie and was introduced to Linc's fiancée, Gemma, and her son, Evan. A lovely strawberry blonde with dark green eyes, Gemma was clearly smitten with Linc. The loving glances and touches between the engaged couple were sweet to see but left a hollow sensation inside Julie's rib cage. It was a future she would never know. A month ago it wouldn't have mattered. But since becoming involved with Gil and Abby, her perspective had shifted.

After a light meal and a sumptuous cake made for the occasion, the family settled in the family room, where Linc had built a roaring fire in the large fireplace. Gemma came and sat beside her on the sofa.

"I'm glad you came today. I was afraid I wouldn't get to meet you before you left. Gil says you've been a big help with Abby's adjustment."

Julie met her gaze. "Gil is a wonderful father. He just needed a little direction."

"I think you're too modest. They think the world of you."

She tried not to be envious of the lovely woman. She liked her, and if Julie was remaining in town, she suspected she and Gemma could become friends. But she had an advantage Julie would never have. "The Montgomerys are a special family."

Gemma's smile softened, and her gaze went to Linc sitting across the room with Gil. "Yes. They are."

Laughter from the brothers drew her attention. Gil's laugh was full and rich, and his smile wide and genuine. It was nice to see him having a good time. At the beginning of her assignment, she'd wondered if she'd ever see him smile. Now he smiled easily, especially when he was with Abby.

The doorbell rang, and Evan jumped up. "I'll get it."

A few moments later Pam Wilson strode in. Julie held her breath. The room went uncomfortably still. What did she want?

The woman scanned the room, person by person, her eyes dark, her mouth in a hard line. Finally she looked at Gil. "I've come to see my niece."

Gil rose to his feet. Abby hurried to her father's side. "What are you doing here, Pam?"

"I told you. I want to spend time with my niece."

He strode forward, gently depositing Abby at Julie's side. "That's not going to happen. You have no right to be here. You need to leave."

"If you think some piece of paper can keep me from my sister's child, you're sadly mistaken. Leah wanted me in Abby's life."

"Leah's gone." He took a step toward her, shoulders stiff. "I'll show you out."

She backed up, glaring. "I will *not* leave until I've had time with Abby."

Abby wrapped her arms around Julie's waist.

Gil straightened. "Linc, call Chief Reynolds, then contact Blake Prescott and tell him we have a situation here. I'm sure you're familiar with the name, Pam. He was my attorney during the custody hearings." He stared at the woman. "His associate in Mobile was deeply involved, too, as I'm sure you recall."

"You can't intimidate me, Gil Montgomery. And you can't keep me from my niece."

Gil stepped forward, took Pam by the arm to escort her from the room.

She pulled away and faced them, her gaze pinned on Abby. "He's not even your father. You're adopted." She glared at Julie. "And I know other things, too."

"That's enough." He grabbed her arm and shoved her into the front hall. Linc followed.

Julie wrapped her arms around Abby, trying to hide her own shaking nerves. "It's all right, sweetie. She's gone."

When Gil and Linc returned a few minutes later, they assured everyone Pam had left. The threat of the police showing up had cooled some of her anger. Gil went straight to Abby and pulled her close. "It's all right, sweet pea. Everything will be okay."

The party was obviously over. Gil muttered a goodbye, promising to fill the family in later. Julie grabbed her coat and purse and followed him, her head spinning. What a horrible conclusion to a wonderful celebration. If Gil's former sister-in-law was like this all the time, she had a new understanding of his dilemma and a new respect for his character.

The woman's comment about knowing something else rubbed like a burr in the back of her mind. She'd hoped she'd misread the woman's scrutiny the day she'd appeared at the house, but now she realized Pam knew, or at least suspected, who she really was. That wasn't her main concern. What would her revelation about Abby being adopted do to her daughter? She had no idea if Abby knew the truth or not. It had never come up.

Gil drove in silence on the way home. Abby curled up in the back with Ruffles. At the house he said good-night, telling Julie he wanted to talk to Abby.

In her apartment, Julie curled up in the corner of the sofa, letting the tears fall. She just wasn't sure if she was crying for Abby, for Gil or for herself. All she knew for certain was that her secrets were about to catch up with her, and she had no idea what to do.

Gil's anger had eased by the time he arrived home but not enough. He wanted to punch something. His jaw ached from clenching his teeth. Like being yanked backward by a bungee cord, all his old resentments and pain sprang to life. He'd believed he'd never have to deal with Leah's sister again. That had been unrealistic and naive. But he'd never imagined she would barge into the family home the way she had and spew her venom.

The important thing now was talking to Abby. As soon as she brought Ruffles back inside, he opened his arms to her. "Are you okay?" She wrapped her arms around his waist and nodded her head against his torso. "I'm sorry she ruined our celebration."

"I don't want to go with her."

"You won't. That's a promise. You're here with me forever. Why don't you feed Ruffles, then get ready for bed? I'll fix popcorn, and we can watch a movie. How's that sound?"

"Good."

He watched her walk from the room, his heart aching and his anger spiking once again. He couldn't believe the gall of the woman. Tomorrow he'd talk with Blake and double-check the legalities to make sure nothing had been missed that might allow his former sister-in-law to claim any rights where Abby was concerned.

But first he had to deal with the woman's outburst about Abby's adoption. He and Leah had always agreed to let Abby know from the start that she'd been adopted, but he had no idea what she had told their child over the last years. Did Abby know? He'd never mentioned it because to him it was a moot point.

His mind filled with ugly possibilities on how she would react, and he prayed their relationship had progressed to the point where it could weather this news.

After placing a bag of popcorn in the microwave, he pushed the button just as Abby came into the room. "It'll be ready in a minute." She wandered into the other room. When he joined her, she was curled up on the sofa with Ruffles. He sat beside her and offered her the bowl. She took a handful of popcorn, her big brown eyes filled with questions as she looked at him.

"I want to talk to you about what your aunt Pam said about me not being your real father."

Abby's lip puckered. "But you are, aren't you?"

"Yes. In every way that matters. But she was right about you being adopted. I want to make sure you know what that means."

"It means you picked me special. Mommy told me."

Tension whooshed from his body. "That's right. We wanted a little girl, and you were the one we chose."

"I'm glad. I love you. And Mommy, too, but she was sick a lot."

Gil braced. He'd have to tread lightly here. "Yes. She couldn't help it."

"I know. It made her sad a lot. But sometimes she was happy."

He pulled her to his side, wrapping her in the crook of his arm. Abby's simple words cracked the hard shell of his resentment. Leah hadn't chosen to be ill, but she had made the choice to keep it from him. That aspect would take a good deal more forgiveness. He wasn't sure he could, but for Abby's sake he'd try.

After tucking Abby in bed, Gil went back downstairs, hoping to divert his troubled thoughts with a good cop show or maybe a ball game on TV. But tapping on the patio door drew his attention. Julie waved at him. He unlocked the door to let her in.

"I couldn't sleep until I talked to you about what happened today."

He nodded. Maybe talking it out with a friend would help him sleep, too. "Not exactly the celebration I'd hoped for."

Julie tucked her leg beneath her as she sat on the sofa. "Is she gone?"

Gil rubbed his forehead. "Yes. She's on her way back to Mobile."

"How do you know?"

"I've got connections. People who'll be watching her and letting me know if she heads this way again. I can't believe the nerve of that woman. After all she did to try to foul up the custody. I should have had Chief Reynolds throw her in jail."

"Why didn't you?"

"I didn't want Abby to see her aunt arrested. Besides, it would only encourage Pam to try harder."

"What can she do? I mean, Abby is your child. I thought everything was settled."

"It is. Legally. But Pam can still stir up trouble. She can spread rumors, and in a small town like Dover, that can become a cancer that destroys from the inside. Most of the ugly accusations she made were kept in Mobile. But if she started saying those things here, it wouldn't only hurt me and Abby, but my family and our business."

"I think she really loves Abby."

He peered at her, caught off guard by her statement. "What does that have to do with anything?"

Julie bit her lip and shrugged. "She missed her. Maybe she just wanted to see her again."

He couldn't believe what he was hearing. "Are you defending her?"

"No. Of course not. But I think I understand what she's going through. And so should you."

Gil squared his shoulders and set his jaw. He was not in the mood to be sympathetic to a woman who had caused him so much grief. "You have no idea what she put me through. She did everything she could over the years to keep me from my child. Used every underhanded thing she could think of. There's no excuse for trying to keep a child from their parent." Anger burned up through his chest, and he clamped his teeth together to keep from saying something rude.

"Or someone who loves them."

Julie's quiet tone pricked his anger. She leaned toward him, her brown eyes filled with tenderness, begging him to listen. He tried to look away, but her gaze held his.

"All I'm saying is maybe you should talk to her and try to work this out."

"No. That's why I got the restraining order. I'll do whatever it takes to keep her away from Abby."

"The way she did to you?"

"Yes." The disappointment in her eyes stung.

"Then you know how it feels. It must have made you angry and desperate."

He searched her face, trying to understand what she wanted from him. Was she turning against him, too? "Are you saying I should forgive her? That's not going to happen. *Ever.*"

"Gil, you're not a hateful man. I've seen the depth of your love for Abby, your devotion to your family, and I've experienced your kindness and compassion toward me. But you are not seeing this clearly. Try to look at it without the emotion."

How could she not see? This was all about emotion. "I lost years of Abby's life because of her. Not to mention Leah keeping her illness a secret. I know Pam was behind that, too. I could have fixed everything if she'd only told me."

Julie tilted her head, sadness reflecting in her eyes. "I doubt that. All I'm saying is that you should talk to her. She's Abby's only relative on her mother's side. Do you *really* want to put her in that position again?"

"What position?"

"Being told hateful things about her aunt the way she was told hateful things about you."

Memories of the pain and anxiety of not knowing how his child was, unable to see her or hold her, flooded through him with the force of a tidal wave. But he had done nothing wrong. There wouldn't have been a custody issue if it weren't for Pam and her selfishness.

"Isn't it time to call a truce and mend the past?"

Old resentments surged to the forefront of his mind, triggering his defenses. "The way you've tried to mend the past with your family?" He regretted the words the instant they were spoken. Julie gasped, her face drained of color.

"That's a totally different situation."

"Is it? It's easy to tell someone else to forgive and take the high road, especially when it's not your pain you're dealing with." He got up from the sofa and strode to the fireplace, staring down into the hearth. He shouldn't have lashed out at her. None of this concerned her in the least. He'd let his bitterness get the better of him. He heard the rustle of her skirt as she stood.

"I was only trying to help. I don't want to see you live your life bitter and resentful. You're too good a man for that."

Shame, hot and condemning, coursed through his veins. He was a jerk. "Julie." She disappeared out the patio door, her image swallowed up in the darkness, leaving a darkness inside him that he suddenly wanted free of.

In his room, sleep eluded him. Even reading a few Scripture passages failed to ease his thoughts. Every verse he selected dealt with forgiveness. Julie had made a good point, but he didn't want to hear it. He wanted to shut Pam out of their lives forever, not make peace. He'd hurt Julie when all she wanted was the best for him and Abby. She'd worked diligently to bring him closer to his daughter. But neither did he want to live with the hate and animosity eating away at him.

He was waiting in the breakfast room the next morning when she arrived. The grim look on her face meant she was still angry with him. Best he swallow his pride. "Julie, about what I said last night. I was out of line. I was upset and angry, and I thought you were turning against me, too."

"No. I understood. Really, I did." She brushed her hair off her face. "Gil, I need some time off. A couple of days."

"Something wrong?"

"My sister has taken a turn for the worse. I really need to be with my family. Do you think you can manage without me? I'll be back by the end of the week."

"Of course. Mom will watch Abby. Take as much time as you need. I hope your sister will get better."

Julie nodded. "Thank you. I'm already packed. Sorry to leave so quickly. Will you explain to Abby for me?"

Before she could leave, he caught her arm and pulled her back around, holding her shoulders in his hands. "Julie, I'll be praying for you and your family. Be careful driving. I want you back safe and sound." She met his gaze, a warmth replacing the worry in her brown eyes.

"I'll be careful. I promise."

"Good. We need you." Unable to stop himself, he bent and placed a kiss on her lips. She reached up and laid her small hand along his cheek and smiled. Then she turned and walked out.

The house had never felt so empty. Neither had his heart.

Chapter Ten

Julie pulled her car to a stop at the small town house in Pensacola, Florida. She'd never been to her parents' new home. They'd made the move from Birmingham when they'd connected with an organization designed to aid families of quadriplegics in need of extensive care. Maryann resided at the organization's well-equipped facility, and her parents had purchased this home to be close to their daughter.

For a moment her courage failed her, and she put the gear shift in Reverse. But the thought of being this close and not seeing her parents filled her with a different kind of fear. She'd closed herself off from her parents too long. It was time to face the past. Gil had forced her to see things differently. How could she advise him to forgive his sister-in-law when she hadn't forgiven her parents?

Please, Lord, give me courage. She had no idea what kind of reception she would receive. Her few phone conversations with her mother had been encouraging, but a face-to-face meeting was different.

With a shaking hand, she knocked on the front door.

It opened quickly. The woman on the other side smiled, her brown eyes widened and her arms opened.

"J.J. Oh, my sweet baby. You're home at last."

Helpless to stop the tears, Julie went into her mother's arms, the years of anger and loneliness melting away. Her mother's hug was warm and forgiving. She was heavier, grayer, but the love she remembered from childhood was still there. How could she have lived without them so long?

"Come in, darling. Your daddy is going to be so happy to see you."

She allowed herself to be guided into the small kitchen, where her father sat at the table. The joy on his face when he saw her sent a new rush of regret coursing through her veins. His hug was as welcoming as her mother's.

When her tears subsided, Julie addressed the next issue. "How's Maryann?"

"Not good, sweetie. The doctors fear pneumonia will set in. If it does, then it'll be a matter of time until the end."

"I'd like to see her."

"Of course. We'll go right away if you want. She'll be so happy to see you. She asks about you often."

Julie raised her eyebrows. Talking was not something her sister could do easily.

Her mother's smile reassured her. "This organization that's helping us has all the latest technologies. Maryann can communicate quite well."

"Mom, I owe you an apology. I've been selfish and angry, and I had no right to be."

Her mother waved off her comments. "We owe you the same. It took me a long time to understand what happened between us." She squeezed Julie's hand. "You must have felt like you'd been tossed aside after the accident. We did everything wrong. I'm so sorry."

Julie brushed tears from her eyes. "Maryann needed you."

"But so did you. Your dad and I were so overwhelmed by what happened and the care that your sister needed. We never stopped to think about how you were coping until after you'd gone."

"There wasn't anything I could do to help, and everything changed. Nothing was the same anymore."

"I see that now. I think we were in shock those first couple of years. When things started to fall apart, we didn't know where to turn. One of the benefits of this organization was counseling. Knowing that your sister was finally receiving the care she needed, and that the costs were being covered, freed us to see what we'd lost where you were concerned."

"I understood, Mom, I really did, but I was all alone with no one to turn to when I needed help." She clasped her hands together. "There's something I have to tell you."

Her mother took her hand and held it tightly. "I'm listening."

When Julie finished telling her about her pregnancy and giving Abby up for adoption, she held her breath, unable to predict how her parents would respond. Tears were spilling down her mother's cheeks, but Julie couldn't tell if she was hurt or angry. "Do you hate me?"

Her mother came around the table and pulled her up into her arms. "Of course not. I'm ashamed that you had to go through that alone, that you felt you couldn't come to us for help."

"You weren't in a position to. I didn't want to add to your burden."

"Hush. You were never that. We could have found a way. And we might have had a granddaughter to love and spoil."

Julie pulled from her mother's embrace. "There's more. And I think I need your help to make things right, because I don't know what to do."

In a way, telling her mother about her position with the Montgomerys would be the most difficult confession of all.

Gil glanced up from his coffee as his mother entered the kitchen. She'd stepped in to watch Abby while Julie was gone. "Good morning." He forced a smile. This was the second morning Julie had been gone, and nothing felt right.

His mother frowned at him. "Aren't you sleeping well? You've got circles under your eyes."

"I'm fine. Just preoccupied with work." The skeptical glance his mother shot in his direction said she wasn't buying it.

"Is Abby up?"

"Yes, but she's moving slowly this morning." His mother headed upstairs, and he took his cup into the office in a feeble attempt to avoid further conversation with his mom. She knew him too well. He hadn't been sleeping. Not since Julie had left. The house didn't feel the same without her. Abby had cried herself to sleep the first night and nothing he could say or do had comforted her. He'd finally offered to let Ruffles sleep in her bed, and she'd settled down.

As for him, there was an emptiness in the center of his chest that refused to go away. He hadn't realized until she was gone how much of his life Julie filled. She was there when he had his morning coffee, when he came home in the evening. She lingered over dinner, joked with him and Abby as they cleaned the kitchen. Even when she was in her apartment, he knew she was nearby. Ruffles had started sitting at the back door each morning, anticipating her arrival.

"Are you trying to avoid me?"

Gil glanced up at his mother, who stood just inside his office. "No. Of course not."

"Abby is afraid Julie won't come back."

"I know. I've tried to reassure her. I reminded her that you came back, and even Ruffles came back after running away. But I don't think she'll be happy until Julie's home again."

"Understandable. She's grown very close to Julie. Things don't feel right with her not here."

"I know. She's become a part of the family."

"Is that a good thing? She's moving away soon. How will Abby feel about that?"

"She'll miss her. Julie has made a big difference in both our lives."

"Care to elaborate?"

He searched for the right words. "She sees the bright side of things. She's always upbeat and smiling. She sees the good in others." Gil worked his jaw. "She thinks I should talk to Pam. Try to make peace for Abby's sake."

"Sounds like a good idea. I dislike animosity within

families. Over time it can destroy everyone. As you well know."

Gil knew exactly what his mother meant. He'd been unable to dismiss Julie's advice. The more he thought about it, the more he knew she was right. "I called Pam this morning. We're going to meet in Hattiesburg tomorrow and talk."

"That's a good first step. But it will take time." She came to his side, giving him a quick hug. "However it works out, I'm proud of you for your decision. I think Julie brings out the best in you. Remember that, no matter what happens."

He had the oddest feeling that his mother's words held a deeper meaning, but he had no idea what it might be.

He was still mulling over his mother's words as well as Julie's advice the next day as he pulled into a parking spot at Chadwick's, the local restaurant in Hattiesburg where Pam had agreed to meet him. It was equal distance between Dover and Pam's home in Mobile.

Gil still questioned the wisdom of this encounter. He held out little hope of reaching a peaceful arrangement, but Julie did have a valid point. It would do Abby no good to have her family at odds with one another. Like it or not, Pam was her aunt. He couldn't change that.

He'd arrived early at the restaurant and requested a table in a secluded corner. He doubted Pam would create a scene in a public place. He took the seat facing the entrance. The sight of her as she came toward him, her mouth pinched into a thin line, triggered his defenses. He fought them down. For Julie's sake he'd be civil and listen to his wife's sister.

Pam stopped at the table, her blue eyes glaring through him. "This is a waste of time."

"Probably." He motioned her to sit. She waited until they'd placed their order before speaking.

"If you've come to serve me with more legal papers, forget it. I plan on filing for custody of Abby. At the very least, visitation rights. Whatever I have to do."

"That's your right. Mine is to protect my daughter." Gil strived to keep his tone calm and reasonable.

"She's my sister's daughter, too. Abby belongs to both of us."

A flash of emotion shot through Pam's eyes. Gil knew the look well. Pain. Pam was experiencing the same kind of pain he had when Abby was cut out of his life. "Yes, she does."

Pam leaned forward, staring into his eyes. "Why do you want to cut me out of my niece's life?"

"Why did you want to cut me out?"

Her expression hardened. "You treated my sister horribly. You never made her happy. Ever. You didn't deserve to see Abby."

"Nothing I did or didn't do would have made Leah happy. You know that." He leaned back in his seat, clenching his fist. "Did you hate me that much?"

"You took her away. You brought her to that horrible little town, and she didn't want to come home anymore." Pam swiped tears from her cheeks and glared back at him. "All she talked about was the wonderful Montgomerys, and how charming Dover was and how happy she was."

The truth flooded through Gil with sudden clarity, freeing him. This wasn't about him or Leah.

"You were jealous." Why hadn't he seen this before?

"Leah was all I had. I raised her like my own child after our parents died. I was glad when she left you and came home, where I could take care of her and Abby without any interference."

Gil softened his tone. "Where you didn't have to compete with anyone for her affections?"

Pam gasped. Eyes wide. "She needed me. I was the only one who understood her."

"That's it, isn't it? You didn't think Leah could love me and Abby and you, too."

For the first time in years Gil took a new look at his sister-in-law. It all made sense. Gil had grown up in a family where love was an ever-flowing fountain. Leah and Pam had only each other, and no one to show them that love was infinite.

"I'm sorry you felt that way, Pam. I didn't understand. We should have talked about this a long time ago."

Pam fought back tears. "It wouldn't have mattered."

"Yes, it would. I would have done things differently. I would have tried harder to make you feel included in my family. I'm sorry."

"I just want to be able to see Abby."

The fear on the woman's face triggered a depth of compassion he didn't know he possessed. "All right. Let's start out with a few short visits. But not alone. I'll be there the whole time. It's going to take time for me to trust you, Pam. We'll take this slow. If everything goes well, we can extend the visits. I don't want Abby to be afraid of you the way she was of me when she came home."

Pam nodded. "We'll try. But I'm not promising anything."

Gil saw a softening in his former sister-in-law's features. He made a mental note to send Julie flowers when she came home. She'd managed to turn a bad situation around with her sound advice. Her wisdom never ceased to amaze him.

Julie pulled into Gil's empty driveway Friday afternoon with a sense of relief. The trip home had been long and frustrating. I-10 in Mobile was clogged with traffic, and the long stretches of empty landscape up Highway 98 had made the trip seem even longer.

A glance at the clock on her dashboard told her that it was almost time for school to let out, which explained the empty driveway. Francie must be on her way to pick up Abby.

Her heartbeat quickened at the thought of seeing her little girl again. It had been only a few days, but Abby and Gil had been in her thoughts every moment.

One saving grace had been telling her parents about Abby. They'd been overjoyed to learn they had a granddaughter, but heartsick to know they'd never meet her. Regaling them with tales of her time as Abby's nanny had helped them all. Though, her mother had urged her strongly to remove herself from the Montgomery home as soon as possible.

She knew she was right. Her departure date for Paris was around the corner. It was time to disengage from her life here with Gil and Abby and step into her real life. Pretending to be part of this one had to stop.

Hauling her luggage up the steps, she unlocked the apartment door and stepped inside, smiling at the welcoming feeling the rooms offered. The tension in her shoulders eased. She was home. Odd how she felt more at home in this tiny little garage apartment than she had anywhere else. With the exception of Gil's home.

The sound of a car door shutting reached her as she tucked her suitcase in the closet. Abby must be home. Hurrying to the door, she opened it as Abby came bounding up the stairs.

"You're back. You came back."

Julie caught the child in a fierce hug, moisture stinging her eyes. How she'd missed her little girl. "It's so good to see you."

"I missed you, Miss Julie."

"I missed you, too, sweetie."

"I taught Ruffles a new trick. She can walk on her hind legs now. It's really funny. Come see."

Julie glanced down at the driveway, her gaze locking with Gil, who stood tall and straight in front of the car. Even across the distance she could read the welcome in his blue eyes.

She drank in the sight of him. The broad shoulders, the pale blue button-up shirt, the dark jeans that covered his long legs. Everything about him sent her pulse racing. He was the most handsome man she'd ever met, but that wasn't what she loved most. His caring and compassionate heart quickened her blood. His devotion to his family and to her child counted more than anything.

He met her at the bottom of the stairs, his smile slowly turning her insides to goo.

"Welcome home."

Her heart skipped a beat. Not welcome back, but welcome home. She was home. She belonged here with him and Abby, but only in her dreams.

"It's good to be…back."

"How's your sister?"

"Stable, but the doctors are concerned. She's getting the best of care, so my folks are taking comfort from that." She glanced at his car. "Where's your mom? Did you pick Abby up from school?"

He took her arm and guided her toward the house. "I had a meeting with Mrs. Taylor. She's very pleased with Abby's progress. She's participating in class more, and her math skills are right on target. She asked me to thank you for your help."

He opened the back door to let her enter. "My mom is busy with Gemma today. Tomorrow is the wedding." He reached out and brushed a stray hair from her cheek, sending a warm rush through her veins. "Abby was afraid you wouldn't be back in time."

"I couldn't miss seeing her toss rose petals down the aisle."

"Good, because I doubt if I could have handled that frilly dress and putting that flowered ring on her head. She needs you for that."

"Someone would have helped her."

"Not the way you can. The place fell apart without you. No one can run the house as efficiently as you do. Maybe I should hire you permanently."

Something inside her broke. She took a step back, breaking eye contact. "Any well-trained nanny could do the same."

"No, Julie, that's not what I meant. Nothing was the same without you here."

"You better get used to it. I won't be around much longer."

"Miss Julie, watch."

Abby hurried into the kitchen with Ruffles, eager to show off her new trick.

Grateful for the interruption, she smiled at Abby, chuckling as the little dog reared back onto her hind legs and hopped across the kitchen.

"That's amazing, Abby. Good job."

Abby hurried forward and gave her another hug. "I'm glad you're home."

"Me, too, Abby." She avoided looking at Gil. She'd been a fool to think his attention was more than gratitude. Playing mommy to Abby had distorted reality. If it wasn't too late, she'd contact the International School and tell them she'd be happy to come early to start her job. It was time to leave. No matter what the cost.

Gil pulled off his sweater and tossed it onto the bed before going into the bathroom to brush his teeth. The wedding rehearsal last night had gone off without a hitch. Since it was a small wedding party, it made for a short evening. Julie had attended the rehearsal to watch over Abby, but she'd refused to accompany him to the dinner afterward.

His reflection in the mirror mocked him. "You really stepped in it this time, Montgomery." His thoughtless comment about Julie's skill in running his home had been one of his more boneheaded moves. He'd meant to compliment her, express how his life had been upside down without her there. All he'd done was relegate her to hired help. He didn't blame her for being hurt. She'd given him the cold shoulder ever since.

Today was his brother's wedding. He would marry the woman of his dreams and become a father. His heart twisted with conflicting emotions. He was happy for Linc. His brother was a terrific guy, and he deserved to be happy. But his happiness only highlighted Gil's growing desire for a complete family, a woman to stand by his side and help raise his daughter. A woman who loved them both.

Picking up the can of shaving cream, he sprayed a glob onto his fingertips. "You are a selfish jerk, Montgomery." He'd asked the Lord to return his child to him and vowed to never ask another thing. One of those negotiating prayers people made when they were desperate. Well, his prayer had been answered, and now he was whining because he wanted more.

Julie had a life of her own. So did he. But that didn't mean they couldn't be friends. As soon as he had a moment today, he'd pull her aside and ask her forgiveness and try to express his gratitude in a more personal way. From the heart and not his practical, clueless brain.

He wanted things to return to the way they were. He missed her laughter, her intelligent conversations and her questions about his work. And yes, he missed her home cooking, too. So sue him. Coming home to a house without her presence left him feeling abandoned. He never wanted to feel that way again.

Clean shaven and dressed in his tuxedo, Gil put Ruffles in her cage and headed out. Julie had taken Abby to the church early to get her dressed and fix her hair. All he had to do was show up and stand beside his brother.

With a few minutes to spare, Gil went in search of Julie when he arrived at Peace Community Church, only to find he wasn't allowed in the bride's room. He sent a message for Julie to step out. She searched his face with worried brown eyes.

"Is everything okay?"

"Yes, I just wanted to see how Abby was."

A bright smile lit her lovely face. "She's adorable."

As if hearing her name, his daughter pushed out of the door and stood in front of him, holding out the skirt of the frilly dress. "Isn't it beautiful, Daddy? It's my favorite dress ever."

"You look like a real princess."

She touched the flower ring in her hair. "Julie fixed my hair. Isn't it pretty?"

"It is."

Julie nudged Abby back into the bride's room, her bright smile revealing her pride and delight. "She's going to steal the show from Gemma."

"I agree. Julie, I wanted to talk to you for a second." Her smile faded, and she stepped back.

"Later, okay? I've still got things to do here. I'll see you at the reception." She turned and went back in the room, closing the door behind her.

There was no way he could misinterpret her actions. The topic was closed for discussion. He'd have to try a different approach. Right now he had a wedding to participate in.

Chapter Eleven

Julie took her seat in the sanctuary, a pew midway down the aisle and on the end so she could have a clear view of Abby as she scattered her petals. The church was empty. Guests would be arriving soon. She'd delivered Abby in her sweet white dress sprinkled with tiny lavender flowers and a wide lavender sash to Francie. She'd looked adorable. Dark hair pulled up into ringlets, baby's breath wreath on her head. Sometimes it was hard to reconcile the timid, withdrawn little girl with the happy one she saw now. For all her anxiety over remaining in Gil's home, seeing her daughter grow more confident and happy made it all worthwhile.

The church looked lovely, decorated with large white floral arrangements and puffy lavender bows accented with baby's breath. The old church with its beautiful stained glass windows, dark wood moldings and historic architecture needed little else to enhance it. A sense of peace permeated the building. If she ever got married, she'd want it to be in a church like this. A small, intimate wedding with only the important people to witness it.

Her gaze drifted around the space, landing on the altar awaiting the happy couple. Out here in the pew, seated alone, the chasm between her and the Montgomerys was more evident than ever. No matter how comfortable she felt with Gil and Abby, how accepted by Francie, she could never be a part of this family. As Gil had pointed out, she was the nanny. Hired help they appreciated.

It was her own fault. She should never have started on this fool's journey. Di was right. She'd created her own mess, and she'd have to live with the consequences.

She barely noticed when the guests started to arrive. She kept her gaze forward and moved only to allow others into the pew. It wasn't until Nancy Scott took a seat beside her that she had to pull out of her troubled thoughts.

Thankfully the music started, eliminating the need for small talk. Every aspect of the intimate ceremony was perfection. Julie's gaze locked on Gil as he and Linc stepped to the pastor's side. Linc looked nervous, his eyes trained on the back of the church, waiting for a glimpse of his bride. Gil looked breathtakingly handsome in his tux. It emphasized his broad shoulders and lean length. Her mouth went dry. He met her gaze and her cheeks warmed, unable to keep from smiling. He smiled back and winked, bumping up his attractiveness another level. The tux only made him more irresistible. Not that he needed any help.

She glanced away as Gemma's sister, Beatrice, came down the aisle in a simple pale lavender tea-length gown and took her place at the front. Abby and Evan came next, and Julie bit her lip to keep from exclaiming her delight. They looked adorable. Evan in a little tux, holding the ring pillow as if it were glass, Abby daintily tossing petals with great care. She'd never been more proud of her little girl. But she couldn't tell anyone. Couldn't share her pride because no one could ever know.

Thankfully the bridal march sounded and the guests rose to their feet, distracting her enough to regain control of her emotions. Gemma was a stunning bride. Her cream-colored lace gown skimmed her trim figure and flowed softly around her ankles. She came down the aisle alone. Julie had heard through the rumor mill that Gemma's parents wouldn't be attending the ceremony. Her heart went out to the woman. Family discord could skew many happy moments.

The ceremony was simple and sincere. Linc looked at his bride with a love that brought an ache to Julie's heart. She would never know what it felt like to have a man gaze at her with such adoration.

Francie had invited her to the reception at the main house. She'd tried to decline, but Gil's and Abby's pleading made that impossible. The wedding ceremony might have been small and intimate, restricted to family and close friends, but the reception had been thrown open to the whole town. That meant that she could slip away after paying her respects. She'd never been good at making chitchat in large crowds.

The wedding party would be staying at the church for pictures, so Abby would be coming to the reception with Gil. Julie decided to go on to the Montgomery home. Maybe she could slip away and take a walk through the lovely old oaks that surrounded the property until Abby and Gil showed up. Then she'd go home and try to put this day behind her.

* * *

Gil caught a glimpse of Julie as she left the church. He wanted to talk to her, to be close to her. She looked amazing today. The deep blue dress that skimmed her figure made her dark eyes sparkle. He'd seen the admiration in her eyes when she looked at him. What woman could resist a tuxedo? Too bad they were so uncomfortable, or he'd wear one every day just to see that look in her eyes every moment.

The photographer called everyone together, and Gil pulled his thoughts away from Julie. He'd track her down at the reception. Abby had made her promise to stay until she arrived, so he had a good chance of getting her alone to talk. He wasn't going to let the sun go down today until he'd explained his thoughtless comment.

An hour later he and Abby pulled into the drive of the main house. Cars already filled the drive and the space around the cottage. Gil dropped Abby off at the front walk, then pulled his car around to the back. Tents had been set up on the side lawn near the small pond on the property. The whole town had shown up to celebrate his brother's marriage to Gemma. It did his heart good to see the support and affection for Linc.

He rounded the corner of the main house, his gaze searching out one slim dark-haired woman. He started in the house but didn't see her. Abby was too busy playing with Evan and a few of her school friends. After wading through the never-ending sea of well-wishers, Gil began to worry that Julie had gone home. He couldn't leave the reception. His mother would be furious, but he needed to talk to Julie.

Making one last sweep of the front yard, he strolled

toward the cottage. His mother had a large flower garden in the area between the main house and the cottage. The azaleas were starting to bloom, and the wisteria arch Dad had built for her was dripping with the lavender blossoms. A faint creaking sound from the garden stopped him. He knew that sound. Dad had tried everything to stop the noise, but he'd never been able to.

The creaking continued. Gil stepped onto the path leading to the arbor, and found what he'd been looking for. Julie sat in the old swing, one hand clutching the chain as she moved back and forth.

"The last place I looked."

Julie jerked around. "What?"

He joined her on the swing. "When you're looking for something, it's always in the last place you look."

She chuckled. "That's because you stop looking."

"You've found my mother's favorite spot. She calls it her thinking place."

"I can understand why. It's beautiful and soothing here."

"Did you need soothing today?"

"In a way. Weddings are always times to look back on our past."

"Or forward to our future."

"It was a beautiful wedding. Linc and Gemma looked so happy."

"They are. He's a lucky man. And she's got herself one special guy."

"Weren't Abby and Evan adorable?"

"She did a great job. I was very proud of both of you. You looked beautiful today."

She scanned his torso in appreciation. "So do you."

He nodded to acknowledge her compliment. "But I didn't track you down to talk about the wedding."

"Gil…"

"I want to explain about what I said yesterday. It didn't come out the way I intended."

"So I'm not a good nanny?"

"No. I mean yes, of course, but you're more than that. Julie, you have to know how important you are to us. You went way beyond the scope of a nanny. You are special, Julie. I don't think I could have reconnected with Abby without your help."

She shook her head. "You would have gotten there. I just helped things along."

"But the difference is you cared. You didn't have to do that. You could have come in, drove Abby to and from school, watched over her until I got home then left. But you didn't. You care enough to find ways to reach Abby. The dog, the father-daughter dinner and talent show, that was all you."

"I didn't want to see you and Abby living so far apart. She needed her father, and it was clear how much you loved her."

Gil reached out and trailed a finger down her cheek. "I've never known anyone with such a caring heart. Not just for Abby but for me. Everyone. I'm glad you're back. I missed you."

"I missed you both, too. But I can't stay forever. You know that."

"Abby won't be happy when you leave."

"I've tried to prepare her. We talk about it, and I assure her that I'll keep in touch."

"Are you sure you have to go to Paris?" The smile

in her eyes faded, and she rose from the swing, send-ing it bobbing on the chains.

"It's something I've worked toward for a long time." She turned to face him, catching her hair in the branches of the climbing rose covering the arbor.

Gil jumped up, gently trying to untangle her wavy hair from the thorns. "Hold still." He stepped closer, slowly pulling the silky strands away from the bush. Her soft whimpers as he tugged on her hair tore through him, and he stepped closer. When the last strand was freed, he brushed her hair from her face, letting his hand linger in the waves. "All better."

She lifted her gaze to meet his, her lips slightly parted in a thankful smile. "My hero."

"It's the tux. It makes women think we're heroic. Even if we're just ordinary guys trying to find our way around."

Julie touched his bottom lip. "You are the most con-fident man I've ever known. There's nothing ordinary about you."

The look in her brown eyes bolstered his courage. Whatever the outcome, he needed to hold her one more time. He slipped his arms around her waist. When she didn't resist, he tilted his head and captured her lips. Her arms encircled his neck as she returned the kiss. Her fingers slid into his hair, and he tightened his hold. He couldn't tell whose heart was beating. All he was certain of was that Julie was meant for him. She was part of him.

Julie ended the kiss, inhaling quickly. "I'd better go."

Gil understood her confusion. His emotions were doing somersaults, too. Before she could move, he cradled her face in his hands and placed one more tender kiss on her lips. "We'll talk again later."

She nodded, then hurried down the path, disappearing into the distance.

Something had changed between them. But he couldn't decide if it was a good thing or a bad thing.

Julie stared out the front window of the Square Cup Coffee Shop Monday morning, enjoying the arrival of an early spring. The azaleas in the courthouse square were ablaze with vibrant shades of pink, coral, red and lavender. Spring had always been her favorite time of year. Her most cherished memories had occurred in the spring.

She closed her eyes. And now she had another one to add to her catalog. Gil's kiss had shaken her and opened a chamber in her heart that had been sealed shut for a long time. The fierce tenderness of his kiss, the sense of belonging she'd found in his arms, had sent her scurrying away, like Cinderella from the ball.

Her emotions had been suspended between supreme joy and deep anxiety. If she were free to love Gil, her joy would keep her floating on air forever. But she wasn't free. She was trapped in an impossible situation with no honorable way out.

"Welcome back," DiDi said as she slid into the chair across from her and smiled.

"It's good to be back. I really missed this place."

"I like that. You didn't miss me. Just Dover?"

"You know what I mean."

"I'm afraid I do." DiDi scowled. "How's Maryann? Did you tell your folks about Abby and about your little nanny project here to check on her?"

"Maryann is touch and go right now, but she's getting the best care possible. My folks and I have talked everything out. I told them about Abby. They're thrilled but sad at the same time."

"Understandable. I'm glad you reconnected with them."

"It went better than I ever imagined. It feels good to be back in the family. I'm only sorry they can't meet Abby. They would adore her."

"You've always known that was how it had to be."

"I know. But that's when the idea was abstract. Now it's very real." Julie shrugged off the sober thoughts. There was no way she could go back and change the past. She had to move forward.

DiDi leaned toward her, looking directly in her eyes. "Facing the truth is always best and far less painful. You might think you're protecting others, or hiding your shame, but all that does is complicate matters."

She lowered her gaze to her coffee. The truth of her friend's words penetrated to her core. She knew she was right, but how would she go about straightening out the mess she'd made?

"Julie, you've got to come clean. You're in too deep to keep this quiet any longer. You're going to hurt the man you love and your little girl."

"I don't love Gil."

"So now you're lying to yourself about that, too?"

"Even if I am, I'll be leaving soon. Another week, tops. Then it'll all be in the past, and no one needs to be hurt at all. Why can't you understand?"

"That's just it. I do understand, and look what keeping pointless secrets does. It hurts everyone."

"It's not pointless."

"That may have been true that first week, but now it's a big old elephant following you around everywhere you go. Sooner or later someone is going to notice, and the truth will come out. Wouldn't it be better if you took charge and revealed the truth on your terms?"

Julie wrestled with the situation the rest of the afternoon. Telling the truth now was too risky. But keeping silent had its own risks.

Tuesday afternoon Julie sat in the family room, replaying the memories she'd collected over the past weeks. Except, the house felt empty without Gil. She missed his strong presence and the sound of his deep, commanding voice that always made her feel safe and protected. She had to be realistic. Her fairy tale was ending, and the sooner she accepted that the better.

Gil and Linc had flown to Houston this morning to meet with Al Thompson, the general contractor who had expressed concerns about the stability of Montgomery Electrical. He'd texted that the meeting had gone well, and he was confident things would turn around for their business. He'd thanked her for her suggestions and said they'd be home later today. She was pleased she could help, but it wasn't his gratitude she ached for. She wanted his love. But that was something she didn't deserve.

She looked up from her tablet when Abby called her name. Ruffles jumped onto the sofa and begged to be petted. Abby plopped down beside her, a big smile on her face.

"Hannah's mom has a new movie for us to watch, and we want our hair to match. Can you braid my hair?"

"Of course."

Upstairs, Julie sat on the edge of the bed, pulling a brush through the dark strands of her child's hair. This was one of the joys of her day. Dividing the dark hair into sections, Julie plaited the first braid, securing it with a colored holder.

Abby pulled the finished braid over her shoulder and examined it. "I have a birthday coming soon."

Her heart swelled. "I know. You're going to be nine on April 4."

"Daddy said I can have a big party at Grandma's house."

"That should be fun." Julie entwined the strands.

"Hanna has a birthday in the summer. She said she'll be officially nine at ten forty-five in the morning on her birthday. I don't know what time I was born."

Wrapping the band around the second braid, she let her mind travel back to the most significant day of her life. "It was two thirty-one in the afternoon. A Thursday, and it was a beautiful spring day. Perfect for bringing you into the world."

Abby looked over her shoulder, a deep frown on her face. "How do you know that?"

Realization stole her breath and sent an icy shaft of horror along her spine. What had she done?

"Yes. How *do* you know that?"

Gil. What was he doing home so early? Every vein in her body burned. Her heart stopped beating. She clutched the brush in her hands, unable to look him in the face. How could she have been so careless? She'd guarded her tongue every moment since coming here, and now one thoughtless comment had shattered everything.

The tension in the room pressed in on her, making it difficult to breathe.

"Abby, go on over to Hannah's. She's anxious to start the movie."

Gil stood like a statue in the room until he heard the back door close. Only then did she find the courage to stand and face him. His eyes were dark as midnight and the hard set of his jaw sent a jolt of alarm along her nerves.

"How do you know the time of Abby's birth?"

She wanted to run, but her body was rigid. Tell him! She couldn't avoid this any longer. Focusing her gaze on the brush in her hands, she forced the words from her mouth. "Because I was there."

His hard gaze penetrated to her core. "I don't understand."

She closed her eyes, prayed for strength then looked at him. "I'm Abby's mother. I gave her up for adoption when she was born." Each play of emotion across Gil's face ripped through her heart like a jagged knife. But it was the look of realization that threatened to buckle her knees.

"You're her mother."

Julie longed to reach out to him, to assure him everything would be all right, but the horror in his voice was forbidding her to move.

Gil ran his hand through his hair as he paced the small room. "How could I have been so stupid?" His steely gaze nailed her to the floor. "She looks just like you. That's why you never wanted to have your picture taken together, isn't it? Am I the only one who didn't see it?"

"Gil, I need to explain."

"What? Why you lied to me all this time? What did you want, Julie? Are you trying to take Abby away from me?"

"No! I'd never do that."

"How do I know that? What kind of game have you been playing? Are you and Pam in this together? Is that it? You've got some scheme to discredit me and take Abby? Well, you can forget it. I'll never let her go."

Julie clutched her throat. "No! No, I would never take her from you."

He turned away, inhaling between his teeth, upper lip curled. "It all makes sense now. The way you bonded with her so quickly. Your devotion to helping her. I thought you were different. Honest. What a joke."

"If you'll let me explain. I just wanted to see that she was all right. That she was happy."

He whirled and glared at her. "She is."

She flinched at his anger but didn't back down. She had to make him understand. "But she *wasn't* happy. It was only supposed to be for a week. I just wanted to see her before I left the country. Then you asked me to stay, and I saw a chance to bring you and Abby together. I just wanted to help."

"Help? By lying to me and my daughter?" Gil rubbed his forehead. "Abby. How am I going to explain this to her?"

"I'll find a way."

He jerked around, his eyes hard and dark. "No, you won't. I want you out of her life. Now."

"But I have to tell her goodbye. She'll be upset."

"Whose fault is that?"

"Gil, she's my daughter."

"No. She's *my* daughter." Gil pivoted on his heel and walked out. "Don't be here when I get back."

Julie sank onto the bed, too numb to cry. Cords of sorrow and remorse curled around her senses tighter and tighter until she couldn't breathe. She clutched her necklace, her one link to sanity. She'd ruined everything. She hurt Gil deeply. He'd been lied to before, and now she'd made him feel like a fool again. He would never be able to forgive her. Ruffles came and placed her paws on Julie's knees. Scooping the little dog up, she buried her face in the soft fur. "Oh, Ruffles, what am I going to do?"

Julie closed her eyes, searching for the words to offer up a prayer for forgiveness and direction, but none came. Only a soft groan of defeat.

Her secrets had finally caught up with her. She couldn't blame Gil for being angry and upset. She deserved it. But what about Abby? She couldn't walk away without some kind of explanation.

Slowly she stood, glancing around the room. Maybe she could leave a note. No. Gil would find it and probably tear it up. Her hand went to her throat. The necklace. It belonged to Abby in a sense. It was the only thing she could give her now. Their link. It was time to let it go. Make a clean break. Unfastening the clasp, Julie draped the necklace around the neck of Abby's favorite doll, propped up against the bed pillows.

Numb and foggy, she made her way to the apartment, absently gathering up her belongings. Each breath tore another section of her heart away. How could she leave the two people she loved most?

She wrestled her luggage down the stairs. There was no handsome man with strong arms to help her this time. Those arms would never hold her again. His smile would never touch her with tenderness.

Climbing into the car, Julie stared out the windshield. Where would she go? She'd vacated her duplex. DiDi and Ed had left this morning for a trip. She'd already turned down her chance to leave for Paris early. Where else was there?

Pensacola.

With shaky hands, she pulled her phone out and touched the screen.

"Mom. I'm coming home."

Chapter Twelve

Every nerve in Gil's body sparked like a frayed wire. He pulled into the drive of his family home with no recollection of deciding to come here. All he knew was he wanted as far away from Julie as he could get. Bands of tension squeezed around his chest. His jaw ached from clenching his teeth. His heart had shriveled into a black cinder. But it was his fear for Abby that twisted inside him like barbed wire.

He stopped the car, clutching the steering wheel and dropping his forehead onto his hands. He was too shell-shocked even to pray. All he could do was call on His name. Pulling himself together, he went inside the house. His mother met him in the hall.

"Gil? What's wrong?" She gave him a hug and urged him toward the kitchen, the place they always talked. After pouring him a glass of tea, she joined him at the table.

He searched for a place to start. "I just found out Julie is Abby's birth mother. She's been lying to us the whole time."

"Oh, dear."

It took him a moment to register that his mother wasn't as shocked as he'd expected her to be. The moment he met her gaze, his gut kicked. "You knew. Why didn't you tell me?"

"I hoped she would."

"She *told* you?" He dragged a hand across his mouth. "Oh, this just gets better and better."

"No. But I had a strong suspicion. The necklace she wore, the little filigree heart. A few months ago a young woman in our Bible study shared her testimony. She told us she'd gotten pregnant very young and had given her child up for adoption. The foundation that helped her gave them each a necklace as a remembrance. When I saw Julie's, I put it together."

He clutched his hands in front of his chin. "Who else knew?"

His mother sighed and met his gaze. "I think Pam figured it out. Linc, too."

Gil exhaled a bitter laugh. "So I'm the only blind idiot who didn't see through her deception? Guess that's a bad habit of mine."

"You saw what you wanted to see. I'm surprised you never noticed the resemblance, but you've always been a trusting person. Have you told Abby who Julie is?"

"No, and I'm not going to tell her."

"Is that wise?"

"I don't know. I'm not sure of anything right now."

"Gil, I've gotten to know Julie a little in these few weeks. She's not a vicious woman. I don't believe she set out to deceive you."

Anger drove him to his feet. He didn't want to hear any endorsements of the nanny. "She infiltrated my home like a spy." He turned his back on his mother, setting his hands on his hips. "It all makes sense now. The way she bonded with Abby so quickly, the way she loved her so much. What a chump I am."

"Because you fell in love with her, or because you didn't see what was right in front of you?"

"Both." Anger spent, Gil sank onto the chair again, hands clasped on the table. "I thought she was different."

"She has a big heart. Julie will be hurt by this as much as you and Abby."

A memory of the agony on Julie's face when she admitted the truth penetrated his pain. She would be hurt, deeply. He rubbed his forehead and hardened his heart. "Not my problem. Abby is. I don't know how she'll take Julie's sudden departure."

"Not well. But how are *you* taking it? I know you love her. And I suspect she's in love with you, too."

"It doesn't matter."

"But it does." She leaned forward. "You know your dad and I loved Leah. As much as she would allow. But we never thought you were right for each other. I watched you grow more and more withdrawn and bitter in the marriage and after the divorce. I understood you were hurting and angry, and desperate to see Abby, but you changed. We worried. After your father died, I worried you'd lost your anchor." She sighed. "Then with losing Leah so soon and the custody battle, you became cold and hard."

She reached over and took his hand. Gil didn't pull away. He needed her comfort and guidance right now.

"Then I came home and met Julie. You were relaxed and happy again. Like your old self. Seeing you with your guitar, you and Abby onstage, gave me hope that you could find peace again. Julie gave you that, and I'm grateful. I can't hate her for restoring my son's joy or for helping him bond with his child. You need her in your life, and so does Abby."

He shook his head. "My only concern is what this is going to do to Abby when she finds out the truth."

"I suspect not as much as it has to you. She knows she's adopted. She's bound to have wondered about her real mother. Finding out it's someone she already adores will be exciting. Learning the truth doesn't have to cause anger and resentment. Sometimes it can bring about healing."

Gil mulled over his mother's words as he drove home. He thought about his conversation with Pam. The truth had cleared a path for them to set the old resentments and jealously aside and work toward a better future.

As he pulled into the driveway, his throat tightened at the absence of Julie's car. She was gone. Probably forever. He should be relieved. But all he felt was a terrible sense of emptiness.

Julie sat in the rocker on the front porch of her parents' town house, battling waves of grief. Her sister's funeral had been this morning. She'd had only a week with her before she passed away. She grieved for the loss of her sister, but also for the lost time together.

"J.J? Are you all right?"

She nodded at her mother as she took a seat in the other rocker. "I wish I'd come home sooner. I'm so sorry, Mom. I could have helped. I could have spent more time with Maryann."

"Sweetheart, there was nothing you could have

done. Believe me. She's at peace now with the Lord. We need to take comfort from that. It's your peace I'm concerned with now."

"I'm fine. I have a bright future ahead of me. I'll get to live in Paris. You and Dad will come and visit, won't you?" The look in her mom's eyes told her she wasn't buying it.

"Julianna. Stop lying to yourself. Haven't you done that long enough? I know you love that young man, Gil. You need to go back to Dover and clear the air with him."

"Mom, he won't listen. Besides, he won't let me see Abby again."

"I'm not talking about Abby. I'm talking about your feelings for Gil. If you love him, doesn't he deserve to know? Doesn't he deserve to hear an apology from you?"

"I tried. He wouldn't listen."

"Then try again. Don't give up so easily. It's time you broke that bad habit."

"What are you talking about?"

"You always took the easy way out of things. Your sister was very competitive. Everything was an opportunity to win. Who could run to the car fastest? Who could finish their lunch first? You never rose to the challenge. You gave in and walked away. You couldn't lose if you didn't participate."

Julie wiped tears from her eyes. She was right. Losing to her sister had been too humiliating. She didn't have the competitive nature.

"Sweetheart, don't let this setback keep you from finding happiness. I don't know if this man will forgive you or not. That's not really the issue. You need to tell him everything. Truth isn't the poison, it's the cure."

"I did."

"Then tell him again until he understands. If he doesn't, then you can at least move forward knowing you fought for what you wanted. How much do you love him?"

"More than anything."

"Then ask yourself, do you love Gil for the man he is, or because he's Abby's father?"

She didn't have to think about the answer. She loved Gil for the man he was. Her feelings might have started because of his love for her child, but his compassion, his devotion to those he loved, would have won her heart no matter the circumstances.

She'd tried to tell herself she didn't really love him. Her feelings for Gil were fleeting, a product of being together so much, of their mutual love and concern for Abby. She'd been afraid to admit how much she loved him because she believed it was hopeless. An impossible Cinderella dream.

But that fairy tale had a happy ending. Maybe her mom was right. Maybe it was time she stopped standing on the sidelines and fought for what she wanted. After all, there wasn't anything left to lose.

Gil Montgomery stood on the broad deck at the back of his home watching Abby as she twisted her swing around one direction, then let it unwind quickly in the opposite, sending her feet and her hair sailing in the air. He chuckled softly. She was going to make herself dizzy, but she looked contented and he didn't want to spoil her mood.

It was the first time since Julie had left that Abby hadn't pouted and shot glares in his direction. As far as his daughter was concerned, he was totally to blame for Julie leaving. He had to own that one. But he was suffering, too. It had been one week, three days, fourteen hours since she'd left his home. He missed her. She'd stepped into his life with her bright smile and her caring heart and shone a flashlight into all the dark corners of his mind. She'd taught him how to love again, to enjoy life again and most important, she showed him how to be a father to Abby.

But there was still a big obstacle to overcome. How to tell Abby about Julie. His mother's words of wisdom the other day had nagged at his conscience, forcing him to take a hard look at the situation. She was right about one thing. Keeping secrets was never good. He had no idea how she would react to the truth, but he'd had enough of secrets. "Abby. Time to come in."

He sat down and patted the seat next to him on the couch. "I want to talk to you a minute. You remember a while back when we talked about you being adopted? I want to make sure you understand what that means."

"Mommy said that the lady who had me couldn't keep me because she was sick or poor or something. So she loved me so much she gave me to you and Mommy because she knew you'd take good care of me."

Gil worked his jaw. He'd been unfair to Leah. For all her issues, she'd been up-front and honest with their child. "That's right. Have you ever wondered who that lady might be? Your birth mother?"

She nodded. "Mommy said when I was older she'd help me find her."

He took Abby's hand. "What if I told you that I know who she is and it's someone you care about?"

"Who?"

He took a deep breath, prayed and stepped out in faith. "Julie." He watched the news play across her little face. Her eyes grew puzzled at first, then widened then a smile slowly spread across her face, wrinkling her freckled nose.

"Really? For sure?"

"Yes."

"Is that why she looks like me?"

How long had she suspected? "Yes. What do you think about this? Are you upset?"

She shook her head. "I'm happy. I have two mommies. One who chose me and one who made me. Daddy, we have to go get Julie and bring her back."

"Sweet pea, you know she's moving to Paris soon."

"No, she won't. She loves me. She left me this." Abby pulled out the necklace hidden under her top. "It's my birthstone. She said this was her most special thing. She said moms never leave their little kids if they can help it. Please, Daddy, you have to find her."

"I don't know where she went."

"Miss DiDi will know."

Julie's friend. She'd mentioned her several times. "Right. Do you know her last name?" Abby shook her head. "Did Julie tell you where she was going when she went to visit her family?" Another shake with a puckered lip. "Okay, I'll see what I can find out. Maybe Stephanie or Nancy will know."

Two hours and a dozen phone calls later, Gil knocked on the door of a charming ranch home in Brandon, Mississippi. He was winging it. He hadn't wanted to risk calling ahead and having Julie's friend stonewall him. Showing up in person had shock value, which could work in his favor.

A tall, slender woman with brown skin and long black hair opened the door. Her dark eyes widened as she scanned him up and down. "DiDi Simmons? I'm—"

"Gil Montgomery. Julie described you to perfection. What are you doing here?"

"I need to find her."

DiDi crossed her arms over her chest and tilted her head. "Why?"

A simple question with no simple answer. "Because, I told Abby the truth about Julie, and she wants her back. She's happy that she's her real mother."

"Smart kid. Well, I'm sorry, but I can't tell you where she is. I don't betray a friend's trust."

"I need to talk to her." DiDi looked into his eyes, searching for something. It took only a moment for him to realize what she was looking for. The truth. "I love her. And I need to tell her."

She considered his words, then stepped back and started to close the door. Gil reached out and placed his hand on the wood surface. "Please."

"All I know is that she went home to her parents."

"Where do they live? Do you have an address?"

"Sorry. I won't tell you. She's been through too much." She started to close the door. Defeated, Gil pivoted and started striding down the sidewalk. He'd have to find another way.

"Mr. Montgomery. Have you ever seen the Blue Angels perform?"

Gil stopped and turned around. "What?"

"You know they're based on the coast someplace. You should check them out. If you need directions, when you get there my friend Mike could help you out." She smiled and shut the door.

What was wrong with the woman? He'd come here for her help and all she did was tell him to watch the Navy Demonstration Team. Back in the car, he started to turn the ignition key. Pensacola. The Blue Angels were in Pensacola. Is that where Julie was? A quick search on his cell phone pulled up a dozen Bishops living in the Pensacola area. Only one was named Michael.

First thing tomorrow he was heading to Florida.

Julie's fingers shook as she selected Gil's cell phone number from her contact list and waited for him to answer. She'd taken her mother's advice and returned to Dover to face Gil and tell him everything. If he was willing to listen. She had little hope that anything would change, but her mother was right. She couldn't simply not participate in this issue and walk away the way she had from her sister's constant challenges. This was too important. She loved Gil. She wanted a future with him, and she was willing to step up and fight if necessary.

"Julie? Is that you?"

The sound of Gil's deep voice saying her name shattered her courage. This was a bad idea. "Yes. It's me."

"Where are you? Are you in Pensacola?"

How did he know that? Had DiDi broken her promise? "No. I'm here. In Dover."

"I was going to come to see you this morning, but

something came up at work. Are you okay? I was sorry to hear about your sister. Why didn't you let me know?"

"I didn't think you'd want to hear from me."

He exhaled a sigh. "Yeah. Of course. Julie, I want to see you. We have to talk. Meet me at the house."

He sounded relieved to hear from her. Did that mean he cared, or was she reading too much into his tone because she wanted him to have feelings for her? "No." She couldn't go back there. She'd never be able to say what she needed to in his home. Too many memories. "Not there."

"All right. Some place neutral. The gazebo in the square."

That was a very public place. But maybe that was best. Neither of them would get too emotional in the park. "All right. When?"

"Give me half an hour. And Julie, don't run off. Please."

Her heart skipped a beat. She wanted to believe the affection, the urgency in his voice. She went immediately to the town square, passing the time strolling through the courthouse park. Spring was in full force now, the azaleas exploded in a variety of bold colors all over the square. Irises bobbed their full blooms around the base of the gazebo and planters scattered along the walkways overflowed with daffodils. The vibrant spring helped ease some of her anxiety, though she'd missed Palm Sunday and Easter, special days she'd anticipated spending with Gil and Abby.

She whirled at the sound of her name being called. Gil walked toward her from the middle of the park. Her heart reached out to him. He looked wonderful, his dark hair stirred by the spring breeze, his long, purposeful stride emphasizing his lean strength. She wanted to run to him, to feel his arms around her and rest her head against his solid chest.

As he drew near, she could see his cobalt eyes were troubled. Her hope began to fade.

He stopped a few feet away, searching her face. "I was afraid you wouldn't come."

"I came back to see you. I need to explain."

He glanced around, then took her arm and led her up into the historic gazebo, taking a seat in the back corner. "I need to talk to you, too."

Julie held up her hands. If she didn't say it now she never would. "Gil, I'm sorry. I never meant to hurt you or Abby. I know it was wrong of me, but I had to know if Abby was happy." Tears slipped down her cheeks, and she swiped them away, hating her weakness. "Please try to understand. I didn't expect to become so involved in your life. I should have left sooner. But I wanted to make sure you and Abby were close, that your relationship was sound before I left. Please forgive me."

"No."

Her heart chilled. Her hopes crushed. She started to rise, but he took her hand.

"I should be asking for your forgiveness." Gently he brushed tears from her cheeks. "I didn't even try to understand. I was blindsided. I should have taken time to listen. It wasn't until you were gone that I realized—" he squeezed her hand "—how important you were to me. To us."

Hot disappointment shot through her veins. *Important.* As the necessary caregiver. The nanny who took care of his child and fixed his meals. He hadn't said the word *love*. She pulled her hand away. "How's Abby?"

"She's fine. She misses you. I told her who you are."

Julie gasped. "Does she hate me?"

"No. She was happy. I think on some level she suspected."

She rested her hand at her throat. At least her greatest fear had been put to rest. "I'm glad. All I ever wanted was for her to be happy. It was the only thing I worried about from the moment I gave her up. When I decided to move overseas, I knew I couldn't leave until I was sure she was all right. That's the only reason I took the job with you."

"How did you know I was the one who adopted her?"

"DiDi found out somehow. I never asked. I didn't want to complicate my baby's life. But I did. I messed it up horribly."

"No, you didn't. You were exactly what we needed. You were our blessing. The person who brought light and joy back to both of us."

She stood. "I'm glad. And I'm glad Abby isn't angry with me. Maybe you'll allow me to see her or at least stay in touch with her."

Gil reached for her hand again. "Julie, of course you can see her. Whenever you want, but I hope we don't have to schedule appointments." He stood and took her arms in his hands. "Don't you understand how much you mean to me?"

She couldn't meet his gaze. "I do. I'm a very good nanny."

He tilted her chin up. "I guess I'm not making myself clear. I love you. I want you to stay here with me and Abby."

Julie searched his eyes, looking for the truth. "I don't understand."

He laid his hand against her face, his thumb gently stroking her cheek. "I love you. I want to marry you. I want you to be in my life forever. Abby wants you to be her mom."

Tears sprung into her eyes, clouding her vision and making it hard to speak. "I don't know."

"Do you love me, Julie?"

All she could do was nod. Through her tears she saw the happy smile soften his features and his blue eyes brighten. He drew her close, slipping his arms around her waist.

"I knew it." He captured her lips, kissing her with an intensity that left her light-headed and dizzy. He held her upright against his chest, deepening the kiss until all she knew was the joy of being in his embrace.

He broke the kiss and inhaled a quick breath. "I knew meeting in a public place was a good idea." He smoothed her hair from her face, then traced her lower lip with one finger. "Will you stay here, give us time to work this all out? I know there's a lot we both have to sort through."

"Are you sure? What about Abby?"

He grinned, pulled out his phone and touched the screen.

"What are you doing?"

He smiled and drew her close again, then nodded in the direction of the park. She looked along the walkway and saw someone running. Abby. And Ruffles.

"Miss Julie!"

Gil leaned close. "She's been waiting with my mom at the coffee shop."

Abby charged up the steps and into her arms. Ruffles barked and danced around her feet for attention. Julie held her daughter tightly, thanking the Lord for giving her a blessing she didn't deserve.

Abby released her and smiled. "You're my real mom. That is so cool."

Julie looked into her eyes. "You're not upset with me?"

"No." She pulled the necklace out of her pocket and handed it back to her. "This is yours. I want you to have it back so you can wear it all the time."

"I don't need it now. I have the real thing."

"But if you wear it, we'll always remember how we found each other again."

Gil took the necklace from her hand and fastened it around her throat, his fingers brushing lightly against her neck. "This will remind us all that we nearly lost something special."

Wrapping an arm about Julie's waist, he held her close. "I think we should pay a visit to Scott's Fine Jewelry soon."

Abby nodded. "And I have to be the flower girl again. I'm pretty good at it now."

Julie snuggled against Gil's side, drawing her daughter into the embrace. A couple passed by the gazebo and smiled at them.

"Y'all make a handsome family."

"This is my mom and dad." Abby leaned against them, smiling.

Julie's heart took flight. Finally, she could be the mother she'd longed to be and give her baby the ideal family she'd always dreamed of. She pressed a little closer to Gil, her pulse skipping at the solid strength of him. "I thought my secret would keep us apart."

Gil tilted her chin upward and kissed her tenderly. "I guess the Lord had other ideas. He sent me and Abby the only woman who would love us and bring us together."

She smiled, basking in the warmth of his nearness. "And He gave me back my daughter."

"*Our* daughter. We're a family now."

"I love the sound of that."

With Abby on one side and her on the other, Gil took their hands and started down the gazebo steps toward home and the promise of a beautiful future together.

* * * * *

Dear Reader,

Welcome back to Dover. Gil and Julie's story is one I've been looking forward to writing for a long time. I wanted to explore how secrets and hidden truths can damage lives and relationships.

Julie Bishop craves reassurance that the child she gave up is happy, so she takes a job as the family's nanny. But things quickly become complicated. As the threat of exposure grows, so does the potential heartbreak for those she cares about.

Gil Montgomery has regained custody of his daughter and has brought her home to Dover but struggles to reconnect with her emotionally after so many years apart. He's also grappling with his feelings of failure as a father and husband. His wife's deception has left him bitter and angry.

Julie never intended to hurt anyone, but as she discovers, the longer secrets stay buried, the worse the corrosion becomes.

Julie and Gil must forgive those who have hurt them and forgive themselves for poor past choices. Only then will they be able to forgive each other and find the happiness they both long for. The Lord shows them that truth is the cure, not the poison, and His grace will cover all their mistakes and losses.

I hope you enjoy Gil and Julie's love story and this trip back to Dover. I love to hear from readers, and I appreciate you choosing to read Gil and Julie's story. You can reach me through my website: lorrainebeatty.com or write me through the Harlequin Reader Service.

God Bless.
Lorraine Beatty

REQUEST YOUR FREE BOOKS!

2 FREE INSPIRATIONAL NOVELS
PLUS 2
FREE
MYSTERY GIFTS

Love Inspired®

YES! Please send me 2 FREE Love Inspired® novels and my 2 FREE mystery gifts (gifts are worth about $10). After receiving them, if I don't wish to receive any more books, I can return the shipping statement marked "cancel." If I don't cancel, I will receive 6 brand-new novels every month and be billed just $4.99 per book in the U.S. or $5.49 per book in Canada. That's a saving of at least 17% off the cover price. It's quite a bargain! Shipping and handling is just 50¢ per book in the U.S. and 75¢ per book in Canada.* I understand that accepting the 2 free books and gifts places me under no obligation to buy anything. I can always return a shipment and cancel at any time. Even if I never buy another book, the two free books and gifts are mine to keep forever.

105/305 IDN GH5P

Name _____ (PLEASE PRINT)

Address _____ Apt. #

City _____ State/Prov. _____ Zip/Postal Code

Signature (if under 18, a parent or guardian must sign)

Mail to the **Reader Service:**
IN U.S.A.: P.O. Box 1867, Buffalo, NY 14240-1867
IN CANADA: P.O. Box 609, Fort Erie, Ontario L2A 5X3

**Are you a subscriber to Love Inspired® books
and want to receive the larger-print edition?
Call 1-800-873-8635 or visit www.ReaderService.com.**

* Terms and prices subject to change without notice. Prices do not include applicable taxes. Sales tax applicable in N.Y. Canadian residents will be charged applicable taxes. Offer not valid in Quebec. This offer is limited to one order per household. Not valid for current subscribers to Love Inspired books. All orders subject to credit approval. Credit or debit balances in a customer's account(s) may be offset by any other outstanding balance owed by or to the customer. Please allow 4 to 6 weeks for delivery. Offer available while quantities last.

Your Privacy—The Reader Service is committed to protecting your privacy. Our Privacy Policy is available online at www.ReaderService.com or upon request from the Reader Service.

We make a portion of our mailing list available to reputable third parties that offer products we believe may interest you. If you prefer that we not exchange your name with third parties, or if you wish to clarify or modify your communication preferences, please visit us at www.ReaderService.com/consumerschoice or write to us at Reader Service Preference Service, P.O. Box 9062, Buffalo, NY 14240-9062. Include your complete name and address.

LI15

SPECIAL EXCERPT FROM

A marriage of convenience for widowed single parents Joshua Stoltzfus and Rebekah Burkholder will mean a stable home for their children. Becoming a family could also lead to healing their past hurts—and a second chance at love.

Read on for a sneak preview of
AN AMISH MATCH by Jo Ann Brown,
available May 2016 from Love Inspired!

"Will you give me an answer, Rebekah? Will you marry me?"

"But why? I don't love you." Her cheeks turned to fire as she hurried to add, "That sounded awful. I'm sorry. The truth is you've always been a *gut* friend, Joshua, which is why I feel I can be blunt."

"If we can't speak honestly now, I can't imagine when we could."

"Then I will honestly say I don't understand why you'd ask me to m-m-marry you." She hated how she stumbled over the simple word.

No, it wasn't simple. There was nothing simple about Joshua Stoltzfus appearing at her door to ask her to become his wife.

"Because we could help each other. Isn't that what a husband and wife are? Helpmeets?" He cleared his throat. "I would rather marry a woman I know and respect as a friend. We've both married once for love, and we've both lost the ones we love. Is it wrong to be more practical this time?"

Every inch of her wanted to shout, *"Ja!"* But his words made sense.

She had married Lloyd because she'd been infatuated with him and the idea of being his wife, so much so that she had convinced herself while they were courting to ignore how rough and demanding he had been with her when she'd caught the odor of beer on his breath. She'd accepted his excuses and his reassurances it wouldn't happen again...even when it had. She'd been blinded by love. How much better would it be to marry with her eyes wide-open? No surprises, and a husband whom she counted among her friends.

She'd be a fool not to agree immediately. "All right," she said. "I will marry you."

"Really?" He appeared shocked, as if he hadn't thought she'd agree quickly.

"Ja." She didn't add anything more, because there wasn't anything more to say. They would be wed, for better or for worse. And she was sure the worse couldn't be as bad as her marriage to Lloyd.

Don't miss
AN AMISH MATCH
by Jo Ann Brown,
available May 2016 wherever
Love Inspired® books and ebooks are sold.

www.LoveInspired.com

*Town founder Will Canfield has big dreams for
Cowboy Creek—but his plans are thrown for a loop
when a tiny bundle is left on his doorstep. With a
baby to care for, the last thing he needs is another
complication. But that's just what he gets, in the form
of a redheaded, trouble-making cowgirl who throws his
world upside down.*

Read on for a sneak preview of
Sherri Shackelford's
SPECIAL DELIVERY BABY,
the exciting continuation of the miniseries
COWBOY CREEK,
available May 2016 from Love Inspired Historical.

"The name is Will Canfield," he said. "Thank you for your assistance, Miss Stone."

"You sure picked a dangerous place to take your baby for a walk, Daddy Canfield. Might want to reconsider your route next time."

The measured expression on his face faltered a notch. "Oh, this isn't my baby."

She hoisted an eyebrow. "Reckon who that baby belongs to is none of my business one way or the other." She gestured toward the child. "I think your girl is getting hungry. Better get mama."

"That's the whole problem." The man spoke more to the infant in his arms than to her. "Someone abandoned her. I found her on my doorstep just now." He glanced over his shoulder and then back at her. "The woman— the one who spooked the cattle. Did you see which way she ran? I think this child belongs to her. If not, then she might have seen something. She was hiding in the shadows when I discovered this little bundle."

"Sorry. I was focused on the cattle."

Clearly frustrated by her answers, Daddy Canfield muttered something unintelligible.

He grimaced and held the bundle away from him, revealing a dark, wet patch on his expensive suit coat.

Tomasina chuckled. The boys were going to love hearing about this one. They'd never believe her but they'd love the telling. Her pa always liked a good yarn, as well. At the thought of her pa, her smile faded. He'd died on the trail a few weeks back and they'd buried him in Oklahoma Territory. The wound of his loss was still raw and she shied away from her memories of him.

"Fellow…" Tomasina said. "As much fun as this has been, I'd best be getting on."

"Thanks for your help back there," Will replied, his tone grudging. "Your quick action averted a disaster."

The admission had obviously cost him. He struck her as a prideful man, and prideful men sometimes needed a reminder of their place in the grand scheme of things.

"Daddy Canfield," she declared. "Since you don't like guns, how do you feel about rodeo shows? You know, trick riding and fancy target shooting?"

"Not in my town. Too dangerous."

"Excellent," Tomasina replied with a hearty grin.

Yep. She felt better already.

Don't miss SPECIAL DELIVERY BABY
by Sherri Shackelford,
available May 2016 wherever
Love Inspired® Historical books and ebooks are sold.
www.LoveInspired.com